ONCE SIGNIFICANT OTHERS

Other Books by Ian Gouge

Novels and Novellas

Tilt - Coverstory books, 2023
Once Significant Others - Coverstory books, 2023
On Parliament Hill - Coverstory books, 2021
A Pattern of Sorts - Coverstory books, 2020
The Opposite of Remembering - Coverstory books, 2020
At Maunston Quay - Coverstory books, 2019
An Infinity of Mirrors - Coverstory books, 2018 (2nd ed.)
The Big Frog Theory - Coverstory books, 2018 (2nd ed.)
Losing Moby Dick and Other Stories - Coverstory books, 2017

Short Stories

An Irregular Piece of Sky - Coverstory books, 2023
Degrees of Separation - Coverstory books, 2018
Secrets & Wisdom - Paperback, 2017

Poetry

Crash - Coverstory books, 2023
not the Sonnets - Coverstory books, 2023
Selected Poems: 1976-2022 - Coverstory books, 2022
The Homelessness of a Child - Coverstory books, 2021
The Myths of Native Trees - Coverstory books, 2020
First-time Visions of Earth from Space - Coverstory books, 2019
After the Rehearsals - Coverstory books, 2018
Punctuations from History - Coverstory books, 2018
Human Archaeology - Paperback, 2017
Collected Poems (1979-2016) - KDP, 2017

Non-Fiction

Shrapnel from a Writing Life - Coverstory books, 2022

Ian Gouge

Once Significant Others

First published in paperback format by
Coverstory books, 2023

ISBN 978-1-7393569-8-9 (Paperback)
ISBN 978-1-7393569-9-6 (eBook)

www.iangouge.com

www.coverstorybooks.com

Arrivals

Sharon

She hadn't meant to die.

Not yet anyway. It hadn't been part of her grand plan, the ambition for a gradual glide into retirement followed by a few years of freedom and greying ease until something unavoidable caught up with her, ideally at a moment pretty much of her own choosing. Which clearly this had not been. In the end it was the unseemly rush she minded most of all. There was nothing gracious about that. It felt as if she were paying the forfeit for a crime she did not commit. Or for something she hadn't regarded as a crime.

All of which left her little room for manoeuvre, and the most important thing became to get the others to come together again, not to see her - it would be too late for that in all sorts of ways - but to see each other. Regarding her initiative more as gift than practical joke, she would be offering them a chance to slay old ghosts, especially as there would be no third parties to interfere: none of their partners would be invited - where they had them - and definitely not Malcolm. Apart from that gathering as her final request (necessarily made by proxy via Niamh) she had nothing else to bequeath.

There had been no ghosts to speak of before the summer of '84, spectral foundations laid across a few short months and built on by arrivals associated with both the annual intake of 'bright young things' at the Insurance company on the other side of the harbour and the opening of a new and temporarily spotless 'logistics hub' on the ring road north of town. For the majority of them - the five others - those early weeks had been brimming with enthusiasm and naïvety in equal measure, the kind of bravado only starting a new job in a new place can conjure. It helped that they possessed an unquestioning belief in the bullet-proof nature of youth; a belief that would be frayed at the edges within three years.

As it turned out, most of them proved themselves to be irregularly shaped pegs sitting unsteadily in perfectly circular professional holes; and if, during those heady first few months they had been swept along by the newness of everything with one or two of them trying to wedge themselves more firmly into their new roles, very quickly it didn't seem to matter. When you overlaid their personal explorations on top - attempts to find out not only who they were but how the world worked and how they might rub-up against others who were similarly floundering - the cocktail was complete. Only Niamh, still there some thirty years later, gave the impression of finding her niche relatively quickly and subsequently sticking with it - though Sharon knows even that assertion is a little superficial. How much of Niamh's perseverance was down to luck or resignation she isn't certain. It - life, that is - proved to be not so easy for her, at least that's how Sharon chooses to frame it at the end. But she also knew it had been hard for each of them; one way or another, they had collectively contrived to make sure of that.

Even if illusory, in the beginning Alan and Simon - revelling in the pretence of the solid and mature aura they seemed determined to project - smoothed the way. Having graduated in different subjects (though all five of them had majored in idealism!) they had walked through the double-doors of the Insurance company's Finance Department as if already privy to its secrets; as if, one day, it would all be theirs; as if they were indomitable; as if there was no way they could ever be ground down by process and routine and the tyranny of numbers. Along with Niamh, equally green in Human Resources, theirs was a triumvirate which coalesced effortlessly, remaining untarnished - for a short while at least - by the personal or subversive. This was adventure in a new world at least two of them were determined to conquer.

Defining where she might sit on the spectrum between victory and defeat was never an issue for Judith, the scales being tipped massively in her favour thanks in no small measure to her remarkable beauty. Right up to the end Sharon debated internally whether she and Niamh ever came to terms with being consistently out-shone by Judith. Sharon liked to think she did - and knew Niamh did not. But was that even relevant any longer? Did it matter? And would the reunion clarify anything, at least for Niamh? Sharon was unable to judge if her assessment was the result of cutting herself some slack and being less self-critical in her final days. But what was the point of beating yourself up when life has already given you a pounding? And as if being tall and slim and perfectly formed wasn't enough, it didn't help that underneath her unblemished exterior, Judith was brighter than all of them too - which made the future into which she would eventually knit herself all the more incongruous. Atypically low-key and unheralded, Judith's arrival at the bank a few weeks after the others had landed in their new world went virtually unnoticed, and it was only her need to house-share with someone - initially Niamh as it turned out - which brought her into their embryonic circle.

In as much as she chose to see herself pulling the strings one final time, the puppet-master dragging her marionettes back for a posthumous farewell gig, Sharon liked to tell herself that she had been the spider at the heart of the web even then. Ignoring the contributions of fate and chance which had transported her from being alone in a clique of one to the master cog in a machine of six, surely she had been at the centre of them all. Already in the town when they arrived - a town in which she had been born and where she worked in the local hospital - eventually she was the only one who remained, apart from Niamh that is. Even if it was a truth with which she played fast-and-loose at times, Sharon had come to appreciate that constancy was worth something, though in her less lucid moments - which became increasingly prevalent as her personal curtain rapidly fell - such a quality came to manifest itself via an elevated opinion of her own importance. If, on occasions of lucidity, she liked to think of herself in the role of organ-grinder, when fully engaged with her decline - and in those few liberating moments when she almost embraced it - she remained savvy enough to recognise that she was, in part, kidding herself. Other than Niamh - who seemed to have inherited at least part of her mantle (and when did that happen?!) - there was no-one left who was qualified to judge, so who cared?

A machine of six? Well finally there was Sebastian, of course. Two years older than most of them, he was the semi-professional maverick partially living off the fame of a father who happened to be a sporting icon. Having already failed in his first choice of career as an architect, he had reinvented himself as a young man emotionally invested in warehousing and logistics, and who - with an enthusiasm which soon betrayed itself as patently manufactured - had sold himself to a company at the heart of the new logistics hub as 'executive material', a talent determined to excel in process efficiency and productivity, a Rising Star who professed to love boxes and pallets and fork-lift trucks and who wanted to revolutionise the industry. Such religion was nothing but veneer. Above all else Sebastian was a salesman, not of things but of himself. That was how he came to them, how he swept them along - as much as Judith had done with her beauty - and how he became, in some senses, the brightest light about which the rest of them seemed to flutter.

And at the end, how did she feel about moths and flames?

Knowing she would not be able to see how they have all been transformed by life, nor vicariously enjoy their reunion, Sharon chose to lay back and wait, to die wondering - and not for the first time - whether there might yet be such things as ghosts; not ghosts of the past, but ghosts of the present. And if there were such things? It was something to cling to, the notion that she might yet act as a witness after all.

§

Niamh

Concerns assailed Niamh from the moment Sharon made her request, one delivered in such a way from the depths of her duvet that made it impossible to deny. "I want them all to come back," she had said, knowing the collective pronoun would be sufficient and that she didn't need to list out individual names. She called it "the last request of a condemned woman". For a short while the two of them had debated the merits of the idea, allowing Niamh to raise practical considerations - or objections couched as such. As long as Sharon remained cogent, Niamh indulged her knowing her friend's position was essentially impregnable. But as soon as she was gone, well, Niamh could act how she pleased - though variation from a pre-agreed course of action would be tantamount to betrayal, the reneging on a contract, and therefore impossible. "I'll be watching" Sharon had threatened with a mischievous laugh that quickly dissolved into a hacking cough, at which point Niamh choose to mime fear as if acknowledging that her friend would indeed still be there, looking over her shoulder, haunting them all.

And why not?

Niamh's worries manifested themselves in the form of questions, and therefore could only disappear once these had been answered. Would they agree to come, in principle at least? And later, no matter what they had previously said or promised, would they actually turn up? When it came down to the practicalities of meeting again as a collective would there be any particular caveats in terms of how they engaged, where they went, even down to the minutiae of who sat next to who at diner? How extant were the various sensitivities of the past? Resurrection of old emotions was, Niamh knew, not only inevitable but potentially disruptive. She had only to consider her own perspective to know that.

And what about their forthcoming meal together? Niamh had to ensure her choice of venue would be acceptable and appropriate; if only 'The Golden Bough' had not succumbed to become an outlet for a coffee chain… In Simon's case there were others who might need to be taken into consideration, not in terms of his attendance but in limiting available dates. His family had blossomed at some point across the last thirty years, though Niamh believed - not without a certain bipartisan frisson - that if the rumours were true, 'blossomed' was hardly the most accurate term to be used in his case. And what if for Judith or Alan there were 'significant others' who begged to come? Or, worse still, children? When she had placed the proposal before them all she had made it as clear as she possibly could that there was only one seat available at the table: the reunion was about Sharon first and foremost, the rest of them came a distant second. From Niamh's perspective, their coming together was to pay tribute to a friend irretrievably lost to them within forty-eight hours of making her last request; any dissection - or resurrection - of the people they used to be should only be regarded as a potential byproduct, not their prime motivation. So there were to be no interlopers. Simon had agreed too quickly. Making reference to his family, he joked that it would "be great to get away from them!" Judith and Sebastian had been slightly more evasive. In Sebastian's case, Niamh exited their initial conversation on the subject with the distinct impression that the pattern of his entire existence remained as 'fluid' as it had always been, such that - even after all these years! - he still found it difficult to pin it down. The way he had quoted "significant others" back to her, heavy with a question of its own, suggested a man whose life was brimming with *insignificant* others, a notion which caused her some pain given all they had been through during that relatively short period they were together. Surely if anyone had been significant in Sebastian's life it would have been them - or some of them, at least?

There had been stories about Judith since the day she left, stories fuelled by second-hand accounts and third-hand reportage. As if no more than an afterthought, occasionally a birthday or Christmas card would turn up out of the blue, always without a pre-printed greeting yet internally dense with Judith's tell-tale small and precise handwriting. If the language occasionally spoke to a narrative of someone in a rush, the delicate cursive script in which the words were written depicted the opposite. On numerous occasions over the years Niamh had seen Judith's photograph in the papers, most often decoratively perched on the arm of a celebrity of some persuasion, the shots taken outside film premieres or nightclubs, or sunbathing on an exotic beach. Her thin slice of fame seemed harvested - inadvertently or not - from the gold-dust rubbed off others rather than as a result of any specific notoriety on her own account: a would-be film star, the lead guitarist of a second-rate rock group, an ageing racing driver on the verge of retirement. Perhaps that was how she had chosen to mine for her treasure, glamour at the slightly jaded end of the spectrum. Even so, Niamh could never quite banish the image of the Judith who left them suddenly that October as being someone about to conquer the world - and on her own terms too. Both gossip and her own intermittent testimony suggested she had accumulated her fair share of scars across the years, probably one for every partner to whom she had temporarily attached herself. Was there someone 'special' at the moment, Niamh had asked? Judith had been evasive, a reticence which extended to her failing to divulge where in the world she had been at the moment of that phone call - something Niamh interpreted as indicating she was either on her way into, or out of, yet another encounter. Time had been kinder to Judith than the rest of them in that her beauty had held up sufficiently well for her to still be slim and attractive - and, Niamh had to admit, sexy - well into her fifties. Over the years her various beaux had moved with the times too, though on a different temporal scale to her own: when she had been twenty-five she had preferred men at least five years older; now she was fifty-five (or was it fifty-six?) her penchant was for partners at least five years younger. Perhaps there had been a synchronisation of ages in her mid-thirties - though Niamh doubts Judith would ever have fallen into the trap of the conventional at any point in her life.

Has she been jealous? It is a question Niamh asked herself during that short period between Sharon's death and funeral - a quiet and deliberately private departure - and the week leading up to their gathering. Sharon had been adamant that they should only come after the formalities were over. Even though it would be irrelevant to her, she had said it would be too easy for them to turn up to play a formulaic role at a funeral and then leave, something which would have defeated the purpose of the reunion. Sharon plainly wasn't interested in 'easy'. After conversations with them all during which arrangements had been drafted and finalised, Niamh found herself variously and inexplicably envious; yet when she examined their lives in turn, her jealousy began to dissolve like early morning mist burned through by the sun. The residue was a smorgasbord of emotions, the most surprising of which is the hope that there are things about her own life the others might covet. Sitting in the deep blue armchair in her lounge - the chair she has loved and cherished for almost half her life - Niamh forces herself to attempt an articulation of her own meagre qualities. Although rapidly abandoned, it was an action akin to putting on a suit of armour before battle.

Nervous as to how their upcoming weekend together will go, she is at least partially reassured in knowing the arrangements themselves are impeccable. Of all of them, who would be better suited to scheduling and planning, to paying attention to the details behind arrivals and departures, the timing of transportations from their various hotels to her house, the cemetery, or the restaurant? She knows precisely where each of them should be at any one moment; all they need to do is to arrive reasonably on time and place themselves in her hands. Such a talent had been nurtured on the back of the structure imposed on her by an Irish Catholic upbringing which, although now two generations removed from the straitjacket of her grandparents' Dublin world, had seen its residue travel to England with her mother and father. When she glances across the room to where Sharon had liked to sit whenever they had dinner in front of the television, Niamh wonders whether she would have assumed such a role had her friend still been alive. Inevitably, the answer is 'not quite'; it would have been more of a joint effort with Sharon doing much of the steering. But in terms of the practical outcome? Either way, she is sure the experience for Simon, Alan, Judith and Sebastian would have been much the same.

Had it been like that all those years ago? Niamh doubts it. She had been less sure of herself back then, more prone to follow, to go where the wind might take her. Not that she is a leader now in spite of her recent promotion - indeed, such a notion has never even crossed her mind. Reinforced by the results of all the personality tests she has ever taken - proof of her investment in her profession - she knows she is simply good at 'sorting things out'. Of course in some respects this imminent project is merely the repayment of a debt. When she had occasionally been at sixes-and-sevens and somewhat adrift, Sharon had always come to her aid, helping her to see through issues (or sometimes around them), often perched on that other chair, coffee in hand, dispensing wisdom. She had been universally selfless, even at times where boundaries became blurred and when Niamh believed her detachment came at considerable personal and emotional cost. That the catalysts for some of those historical events - particularly Sebastian! - are to be arriving in the next few days is perhaps the primary cause of Niamh's nervousness; not because she is worried that she might regress into the person she had been thirty years earlier, but rather because the person she is now might take the opportunity - in an unplanned and impulsive way, which would be so unlike her! - to engage as she should have back then. Yet is there any need to do so, to set the record straight, to right wrongs? Are there any truths to surface or ghosts to slay on her part? Or for any of them, come to that? She tells herself that, if so, at this precise moment it would have been useful to have had the benefit of Sharon's counsel one final time, someone to set expectations, to 'mark her card'. Niamh tries to imagine Sharon's knowing smile, the way she used to incline her head when she was listening hard, the pauses she would insert into her replies in order to ensure the response given was the precise one she wanted to deliver. But just now the other sofa offers nothing but a void - and one that will soon be filled by those once significant others.

§

Simon

"We always said we'd go back, didn't we?" Sounding eerily the same as it had when they first met, Alan's voice comes to Simon via his telephone handset.

"Yes, of course we did. But I never thought anyone actually meant it. It's the kind of promise people make whether they intend to keep it or not."

Having made his observation, Simon stares at the unadorned kitchen wall as if doing so might enable him to conjure up the image of a man he hasn't seen for some considerable time. Has it been too long? Undoubtedly. But if so, isn't that just another example of people not doing what they said they would? "We must get together soon!", words they had all probably uttered at one point or another - although if Simon and Alan had exchanged them when they had last met in London it would have been with little sincerity on either side.

How does Alan look now? The phone offers no clue. Fundamentally the same, Simon assumes, though potentially on the slide now that middle age has begun to assail them all; a little less hair perhaps, or some greying at the temples. Although it had been some years earlier, he wonders if he had seen the first signs of decay that evening in London. Alan had never been the most decorative of specimens, even in his prime, and though Sharon had seen something in him for a while, Simon believes he understands why it had turned out to be insufficient - after all, she proved herself not impervious to the lure of a potentially better offer.

Alan is speaking again.

"I suppose it is. But surely this is a little different; exceptional circumstances and all that. It's not as if we'll be getting back together under false pretences or on a whim of some kind, is it? There's a real and important reason for us to be going back."

Simon tries to interpret what Alan is saying; not the words he is using but rather the way he shapes them, their true meaning bound-up in the manner of their delivery. He is unable to totally reconcile 'real' and 'important'. Of course, Alan has a right to be upset - surely they all have - but all these years later, how hard had he really been hit by the news about Sharon? Or impacted himself, come to that? Even setting that aside, Simon wonders what might lie behind his own instinctive reluctance to return to the scene of so many earlier crimes, to a vaguely soporific seaside town where they had once coalesced, all six of them in their twenties, idealistically and naïvely determined to find their place in the world. Perhaps his reticence is predicated on a fear of reliving of the past; either that or he is somehow daunted by the threat represented by reacquaintance with the very people who had shaped it.

Although he concedes how Alan may have more reason than most to argue for their collective return, the simultaneous absence of Sharon seems to disqualify it. They are to be going back for her, and yet she will not be there.

"Is everyone going?" he asks, assuming Alan is closer to Niamh and therefore is more likely to have his finger on the pulse.

"Yes, as far as I know. Niamh is planning for us to go to the cemetery at some point on the Saturday - early afternoon I think - and then out for a meal in the evening. I think she wants the latter to act as a sort of memorial service, the chance for us to pay tribute as it were. Having looked at all the options, I've decided to go down the night before; that seems the most practical thing to do. I'm booked into that little hotel across the water; you know, the one we briefly stayed in all those years ago. It seemed quite glamorous then I think; I remember feeling quite important."

Simon says nothing in response.

"I assume that's where you'll be too? I think Jude may be staying with Niamh, but I'm not sure."

"And Seb?"

"I've not heard from him myself, but Niamh says he promised to be there. She wonders if he took the news harder than anyone else."

"*That* I find hard to believe" is what Simon wants to say but manages to check himself. Instead he offers "It was probably a shock to all of us" - immediately unsure as to why he had inserted 'probably'. It feels unnecessarily uncharitable.

Alan doesn't respond.

"I'll need to check with work; you know, my diary and things. If I can get down before Saturday, I will."

§

Alan

As soon as he puts down the phone, Alan finds himself wondering why his erstwhile friend had seemed so reluctant about returning to pay his respects to Sharon. Considering past history, there can be no such hesitancy on his side. Whilst it is true that he and Simon had never entirely seen eye-to-eye - thanks, in part, to their radically different outcomes in relation to Sharon herself - there was nothing in any subsequent disagreements to warrant hesitancy, at least as as far as he is concerned. In addition to Simon's one-time feelings for Sharon - and irrespective of their depth, shallow or otherwise - Alan believes he is aware of the tenor of Simon's various relationships with the others, not that those should really be under consideration at a moment like this.

Walking into the small lobby by the back door to change into his gardening shoes, Alan catches a glimpse of his old wax jacket hanging behind one of his lighter coats. It has weathered remarkable well, all things considered; in many ways, better than he has himself. A present from Sharon on their one and only proper Christmas together, Alan can only think of her with fondness - in spite of the way their relationship ended. He is happy to adopt this overtly positive viewpoint as the filtered remembrance of a former optimist, an approach which permits him to accentuate all that was good about the year and a half they were a couple. Gradually they had been nudging towards longer-term commitment right up until those few late summer months when Sebastian seemed to implode, sucking them all into his chaos as if he were a Black Hole from which none could escape. Consequently, if there is any element of the forthcoming reunion about which Alan has reservations it is the prospect of seeing Sebastian again. Finding himself on uncertain ground, he attempts to secure his position by telling himself that, rather than the reunion surfacing any question of forgiveness - or of not forgiving, come to that - his nervousness springs from a vague trepidation as to the potential dynamics for which Sebastian might once again prove responsible, however inadvertently. The two of them have spoken infrequently in the thirty years since Sebastian's leaving party in '88, and although it had been a cause for celebration on a number of fronts - not least the departure of the group's most unstable element - it also represented, if not the beginning of the end (had Judith's departure two months earlier actually signalled that?), then at least confirmed everything was about to change. Their collective exchanges since then, though increasingly sporadic, had been civil enough, often laced with suggestions that they should try and 'get together' at some point, ambitions shared liberally between them and yet - to the best of his knowledge - only very rarely acted upon. Eschewing the wax jacket in favour of a fleece, Alan finds himself trying to imagine the myriad subsequent conversations which had presumably been played out at some point or another between them all; perhaps in every case the general tenor of the dialogue would have been identical, but the words used subtly different.

It had been that way with Simon, although in their case they had actually managed to meet thanks to Niamh. A little over two years after they had dispersed, she told them she was going to be on a training course in London for a few days and had an evening free, so wouldn't it be nice to get together for dinner? The capital had been the place to which both he and Simon had independently gravitated, and where Sebastian and Judith occasionally trespassed. Having always had a soft spot for Niamh (perhaps as the sister he'd never had and always wanted) Alan found it easy to agree to her proposal. Whether or not Simon is now reticent to return to pay tribute to Sharon, Alan's analysis of his attitude is largely shaped by his experience of that evening in London, the two of them forced together without any mediation, compromised by Niamh having to cry-off at the last minute because of an unexpected work commitment. Thinking about it as he slips his arms into the fleece - both the evening itself as well as the events during the years which led up to it - Alan believes he can understand Simon's hesitance, at least in part, after all he has history with each of them.

Opening the back door and beginning to walk down the garden towards the shed (having bullied himself into a little weeding of the borders in order to clear his mind), Alan is struck by how all their narratives were intertwined, like roots mingling beneath the surface of the soil. It proved a weave running the full gamut of emotions; a compendium of interactions which, one way or another, stretched and tested each of them. Because of his own relationship with her and the loyalty that still commands, he likes to think Sharon was sublimely at the heart of things, and in consequence that they all have an outstanding duty to her, even after her passing. It is this belief he uses to justify them coming together again, for his lobbying on Niamh's behalf, and in championing her idea - even though he cannot help but suspect that Sharon is somehow still behind it.

Niamh

Looking over the arrangements for what she hopes will be the last time, Niamh checks the kitchen clock as if to reorientate herself against the timetable. It is an unnecessary activity. In front of her is the single sheet of paper that heralds much, though whether positive or negative she cannot say. If she leaves it there, naked and face-up, staring at her every time she goes to make tea or take a biscuit from the National Trust jar in which she keeps them, it will continue to lure her and she will inevitably re-scan the columns - one for each of them - and the limited number of rows - one per significant chunk of time - in order to revalidate their synchronisation. Having never giving herself credit for even a modicum of imagination, she still tries to envisage them arriving at the station, or checking in at the hotel, or in the taxis that will bring them to her, the cemetery, the meal. And to Sharon. She knows there is unlikely to be anything radically new in these soft collisions, yet can't help but be reminded of when such things were original and fresh.

Hardly Orwellian, 1984 had been a year with beginnings crammed into the space of just a few weeks. The six of them had been like molecules let loose in a brand new Petrie dish, colliding and reacting, binding with each other in order to test out their chemistry as if they were the subjects of some vast experiment. Three years later the dish was no longer pristine; it had become partially fogged by their various fusions, in various places hosting substances that looked vaguely unsavoury, tangible residues which had started to mould. She had seen many such dishes in the labs at the hospital either lined up in military precision across whole benches or loafing in isolated ones or twos near computer screens, stained mugs, and wedges of printout. After the insurance company, working in St Hilda's came as something of a shock; the move from quiet order to bustling disorder took her by surprise, partly because the latter jarred with her nature, and partly because she had assumed if order and control was needed anywhere then it had to be uppermost in healthcare. Not that it affected what she did. "HR people can work anywhere," Sharon had told her, "and we need more good HR people". So an introduction had been made and an interview attended; soon enough she and Sharon were going to work together, and then - trading-up on the strength of their joint salaries - sharing a better house. With the exception of 'the Malcolm years', it was a model which fitted them hand-in-glove for nearly three decades, in an unspoken way dissolving the pressure to seek any alternative domestic template. Until, of course, the day Sharon wasn't there at all. As yet Niamh has been unable to dispel the vague sense that she has lost half of herself - and remains uncertain as to whether or not she needs to find something to fill the void.

The move - both to the hospital and the shared house - happened the year after everyone had abandoned them. Being the only two of the cabal left, to this day Niamh is uncertain whether Sharon's suggestion about her working at St Hilda's and them moving in together was made because she could see Niamh was in need of a fresh start or because she required one herself. Perhaps Sharon recognised the imperative of reliable companionship - though not being one to demonstrate weakness, she had never displayed any indication that the latter was ever in play. As Niamh reflects, she wonders whether, of all of them, Sharon's existence in the mid-eighties had been the most serene. When they arrived, she was already professionally settled, working in the hospital, and her domestic arrangements perfectly stable. Not only that, her embarking on a relationship with Alan a while later invested an air of worldly wisdom in her. Although only marginally older than the rest of them (except Sebastian), for a while she exuded an almost matronly superiority. If you needed counsel or advice you asked Sharon. While this was especially true for Niamh (and very occasionally Judith) in the early days it was not unknown for the boys to also avail themselves of her opinion. Niamh wonders if it is strange that - in spite of his relationship with her - Alan failed to have any of Sharon's maturity rub off on him. He was always the junior partner where Sharon was concerned, and even in the brief tussle with Simon for her affections, remained subservient. It would have probably been the same for Simon had Sharon settled on him as first among equals, yet Niamh believes she can now see - even if she did not at the time - why her friend made the choice she did. And of course, she has even more reason to understand why Sharon separated herself from Alan getting on for two years later. How could she not considering the trigger for doing so turned out to be a trap into which she had subsequently fallen herself? She takes one final look at the sheet on the table, notes the physical proximity of the three columns headed 'Alan', 'Simon' and 'Sebastian', and again wonders whether Sharon, in one final act of practical-jokery, had chosen to light the blue touch-paper.

§

Judith

It is only when she leaves the motorway and passes the sign telling her she has less than twenty miles to go that the prospect of the weekend ahead fully assails Judith. It was a route she frequently used to travel back then when she left the peninsula to visit some of the bank's other branches, or took the coast road east to visit her mother who remained resolutely ensconced in her splendid cathedral city, still trying to age gracefully and fit into the place she had chosen to call home. That the house she had once shared with her daughter was located 'on the wrong side of the river' was a subtlety known only to the locals, and whenever Judith shared her home town with new acquaintances - as she had when meeting Sharon, Niamh and the rest for the first time - she needed only to mention its name to elicit positive comments bordering on envy. "That must have been a wonderful place to grow up!" Invariably its legendary picture-postcard image guaranteed a kind of awe. The post-motorway road sign she has just passed, apparently unadulterated even after all these years, is a trigger sufficient to release a flux of memory and emotion which she spends the next mile or two trying to filter and categorise, all the while preoccupied with the practicalities of the journey - namely her driving (which has never been that proficient) and the scanning of her surroundings in order to see where old things used to be and now new things are. Apart from Niamh - who, to the best of her knowledge, has subsequently never lived anywhere else and is seemingly unperturbed by the constraints of there being only two roads in and out of the place - Judith assumes this returning will be the same for all of them: a challenge of recollection. She feels as if she is about to be tested, asked to weigh her life against some kind of scale in order to determine on which side the balance will be tipped.

There is no doubt she will arrive well-armed. Since they were last together - at *her* leaving party, of all things! - she has lived a life she likes to categorise as being one of Romance, Travel and Adventure, each endowed with capital letters. She is as certain as she can be that none of the others will have seen as much of the world nor enjoyed the same breadth of experience: who else will have played the casinos in Monte Carlo, attended the Grands Prix in São Paulo, seen Machu Picchu, swum the Great Barrier Reef, camped in the Sahara, watched the Northern Lights from the comfort of a Lapland ice hotel? Certainly not Simon or Alan. As she pulls up at a set of traffic lights she finds herself struggling to recall tangible evidence of their possessing any semblance of an adventurous side. Uncharitably or not, nothing comes to mind, apart from Simon's brief, ridiculous and inevitably doomed pursuit of her. Sebastian is an entirely different matter, of course; not simply because she had been closer to him than the others, but because his privileged background is well known and his history, subsequent to her leaving, opaque. Always drawn to an exploration of the unusual and with the instinct to be impulsive (in so many ways!), if she chooses to be charitable Judith can imagine Sebastian in exactly those same places she has been: she can see him in a sharp tuxedo playing roulette wheels or striding sand dunes in khaki and shades. Indeed, there had been a time before they went their separate ways that she and Seb might have shared such a future. Yet even if in the last thirty years or so he *had* been to those same places and had similar experiences, Judith is comforted to know that he would not have been able to do so with her grace or elan. Sebastian's approach would have been more rudimentary, a little rough-and-ready. If she was *Vogue*, he was *Boy's Own*.

Even having reestablished her superiority, Judith remains nervous about the encounter to come, not specifically with Sebastian - though that will have its own challenges - but with them all as a reconstituted group. She fears the dynamic of the collective. Her inherent self-confidence is based on unquestionable superiority when compared to them on a one-to-one basis. For example, is she not more attractive than Niamh? Does she not remain, as she always has been, the most intelligent of the group - and especially so now they are to be deprived of Sharon's somewhat unnerving wit? Yet taken together, is it not possible that by joint force of will they might at some point scratch at the veneer of Monte Carlo or Formula 1 and ask the harder questions as to how she came to be there, what price she had to pay to do so? Judith likes to believe she is well aware of her public image and how the hoi polloi might view her; indeed, how can she not be given she has deliberately cultivated a significant proportion of that image herself? And yet there remains a nagging suspicion that her interpretation is likely to be different to those who are *not* her - and even worse, to those who know her of old. She has become so much more 'rock and roll' than she had been back then. As she passes another sign further counting down the miles to Niamh's house, the certainty of an alternative view - vaguely articulated or otherwise - becomes the dominant factor; yes, she will be able to wow them with tales from her adventures and make them jealous of her lifestyle, but she knows such an opportunity could come at a cost. There may be uncomfortable moments when she will need to be on the defensive - and perhaps Sebastian will be the most active aggressor.

Finding herself slightly out of kilter, when Judith sees a sign for a Starbuck's drive-thru she makes a decision which results in a less than textbook driving manoeuvre, breaking far too late and foregoing any attempt at signalling in order to swerve into the café's short feeder lane off the main road. The driver of the car behind offers her a blast of his horn, something she dismisses as irrelevant. "I've driven in Italy," she tells herself, as if that excuses just about anything. When she pulls to a halt and winds down her window to order a flat white, she notices a flash of recognition on the face of the young man who takes her order. It is a look to which she has become attuned; it tells her that, even if he cannot remember her name or exactly where it was he saw her, he *knows* he has seen her before. Or wishes he had. Judith likes to think it is more than her flawless complexion, the professionalism behind hair and make-up, the cut of her Gucci jacket or the flashiness of her BMW coupé which prompts such a look; she wants there to be an aura about her, one that forces acknowledgement even when there is no familiarity to support it. When she left this small coastal town for what was supposed to be the last time and headed for - according to her own assessment - a stellar modelling career, she'd surely had it then, the 'je ne sais quoi' that allowed her to stand out, and which proved invaluable in opening so many doors. Both literal and metaphorical. Parking-up to sip her coffee, she likes to regard these little encounters - such as the one she has just had - as offering mutual reward: the young man will have a story to tell his friends in exchange for gifting her some positive affirmation. Perhaps his heart may have skipped a beat too. It had been known.

§

Alan

As soon as his feet find the platform Alan pauses and, even though he knows precisely where he is, cannot help but glance inquisitively in the general direction in which everyone is heading. There, some thirty yards ahead of him, the unmistakeable form of Simon, slightly taller than most other passengers, already charging towards the exit. He must have been travelling in a carriage closer to the front of the train. The distance between them is not too great to prevent Alan from calling out Simon's name, to brave the inevitable glances from some of the other travellers, and, on hearing it, for Simon to stop, turn, and acknowledge him with a wave of a hand.

But Alan does no such thing. Instead he looks down at his small suitcase, checks that the handle is extended to its full length, then, after putting his hand into his jacket pocket to verify - once again - that he has his ticket ready for the barrier, pats his trouser pockets to ensure he still has his keys, his wallet. It is a common enough ritual, and in this instance it offers sufficient pause to allow Simon to gain another forty or fifty yards on him, distance enough to erect an invisible barrier to shouting, a buffer that will be populated by bodies at the station exit, and - if Alan has judged things correctly - give Simon time enough to walk up to the harbour-side hotel and have checked-in and gone up to his room before he gets there. As he strolls forward, allowing himself to be overtaken by those more impatient than he, Alan's analysis as to why he failed to arrest his friend's progress takes little time: though not exactly unprepared, he knows he is, as yet, unready. The weekend will be about such comings together, and the 'how' those meetings are executed has perhaps assumed a disproportionate importance for him. He has studied Niamh's schedule almost to the point of memorisation (the whole thing, and not merely the column headed with his name) and inserted himself into the minutiae of each prospective event, imagining as best he can the consequence of every one. Nowhere in Niamh's plan did it say he should accost Simon at the railway station and re-engage him there, therefore he does not.

Slipping his ticket into the barrier for it to then open abruptly, he propels himself forward to pause again once he is through. Now perhaps a hundred and fifty yards ahead, Simon is still moving on at pace, his long and slightly belligerent stride - visible only in embryonic snatches when they had been younger - driving him forwards. It is, Alan thinks, not the movement of a man keen to get to his destination quickly but rather that of a person who wants something out of the way, as if the walk itself is an intrusion only just to be borne. Having seen hints of that burgeoning trait when they had last met all those years ago in London, Alan wonders if that is how Simon now approaches most things, a disgruntled air of impatience become his trademark. If so, it will be interesting to see how he copes with Judith and Sebastian - assuming the latter actually bothers to turn up. Simon hadn't always been like that of course, and Alan cannot help but assume persistent disappointment must have played a hand in his evolution. It is feasible, of course, that Sharon had been the first to introduce Simon to the harsh reality of things not turning out the way he wanted. Not exactly innocent himself, maybe they'd all played their part one way or another, gradually forcing him to abandon the persona of the cheerful graduate who had come to them full of optimism following three years of freedom at Sussex. Like many, he had been a young man who had revelled in being released from the bonds of adolescent constraints into an environment where he could potentially blossom.

Remembering his own unremarkable childhood where university was just the next step on an inevitable treadmill, Alan is certain it had not been like that for them all. He knows relatively little about Niamh's or Judith's upbringing (other than it had, for one reason or another, been less than ideal domestically) and even less about Sharon's - a fact which still astounds him. It is Sebastian who, as a child, was the one moving in entirely different spheres; not that doing so necessarily made him happier. Being the son of a famous international rugby player who on retiring became - and continues to be - a media darling, Sebastian's familial orbit was entirely different. Whilst University proved temporarily liberating for Simon and an environment in which Judith could either find or create herself, Alan had always assumed that for Sebastian it was another something else to which he felt entitled - an assumption which Sebastian himself never did anything to debunk. Perhaps this had been an uncharitable assessment, but Alan can't help but think Sebastian's subsequent challenges with 'the real world' offered conclusive proof as to the veracity of his notion. In his own case, three years at Warwick represented just another test of stamina for a wheel-bound hamster - though the wheel itself had been lubricated and the cage in which it was housed gilded just a little more. He knows the links between their various academic experiences and how they may be today are debatable and tenuous, but aren't they all composites of everything that has happened to them? As Alan recommences his walk away from the station - not quite literally in Simon's footsteps - he is painfully aware of how uneventful his own life has been in comparison to Judith and Sebastian - though perhaps that is true for the rest of them too.

§

Simon

Whether as a byproduct of clever photography or more rudimentary trickery, hotel rooms never live up to the promise they lure you with on the internet; at least that is Simon's theory. One of Life's many universal truths. As he stands in the centre of his smaller-than-expected room, his luggage unopened on the bed, he remembers 'The Nelson' well. Apart from a lick of paint, the foyer is exactly as it had been all those years ago when he had come to the town for the first time, staying overnight in order to prostrate himself before the insurance company's 'Graduate Assessment Centre'. And although the hotel staff have obviously changed since then, he is convinced the latest batch of recruits have already been introduced to that specialist niche of customer service which majors on slovenly disinterest. Perhaps they too had suffered their own version of corporate induction. All of which leaves him unsurprised to find the rooms much as they had been years before and being attended by staff who didn't seem to care that much about him.

After poking his head into the en suite to confirm that it was inevitably and regrettably fitted with a shower and no bath, Simon walks the few paces required to reach the window and looks out. Three floors up - "I'm afraid you'll need to take the stairs as the lift is currently being serviced" - the harbour opens out before him, much as it had in 1984; a semi-busy scene with various ferries plying their trade, and naval vessels attempting to look innocent and unthreatening in their monotone grey. He feels as if he is trapped in a time warp, and wonders if he had occupied this self-same room when he had been thirty-four years younger. Immediately beneath his window a few people zig-zag about on the pavements, cars and buses pause and pulse along the road, and from the station entrance the odd straggler makes their way towards a final destination. At the pedestrian crossing he notes three people waiting for the lights to change in their favour. One of them is Alan. Even though nearly twenty years have passed since they last met in person and with Alan now appearing professionally middle-aged (a transformation already underway in the early nineties), Simon finds him unmistakable. Perhaps they had been on the same train? Simon's weighing up the likelihood of such a coincidence is made less relevant by the intrusion of the bustling scene and a preoccupation with how things in general may - or may not - have changed.

Having watched Alan traverse the road at which point he immediately disappears - presumably to breach the hotel's threshold - Simon turns, slips off his coat with a sigh, and tackles his unpacking. It is a brief and familiar enough ritual: a few things into the top drawer of the low-quality desk-cum-bureau; the wrestling with hangers from the doorless wardrobe in order to minimise creases in two fresh shirts, a pair of trousers, and his jacket; the extraction of essentials from a full wash-bag, and then their migration into an en-suite in which not even a kitten could be swung. Although a simple and predictable performance, perhaps it is also a trailer for the disappointment the next two days may bring. Having already travelled with limited expectations, Simon cannot help but wonder what will be materially different since he left toward the end of the eighties; not in the place so much - if the hotel is anything to go by, the fabric and landscape will surely be pretty much the same! - but in them as a group, as individuals.

Disinclined to begin any speculation with himself as the central focus, as he turns his attention to the scant offerings of the tea-and-coffee tray Simon discovers the only person he can start is with Sebastian. There he expects to see nothing different. "Once a public schoolboy, always a public schoolboy" he says to himself as he walks the kettle through to the sink to fill it with water. Having said that, he tries to take comfort in the almost certain knowledge that Sebastian will be a little dog-eared by now, presumably much like the rest of them. Even so, he remains unable to comprehend how Sebastian can possibly exist as anything other than a concoction of boyish and slightly effete charm: the semi-professional 'Good-Looker' who managed to do so much damage during those final few months. Not that Simon has any particular reason to feel for Niamh or Judith. Nor does he see the need to leap to their defence; after all, he did no such thing in '88 when he had already been relegated to the role of observer, so why should he start now? Sharon and Judith had already combined to ensure his sidelining, the upshot that - unbeknownst to the rest of them - he had already begun applying for jobs elsewhere during those early Summer months. They, the town, and the insurance company had collectively run their course. He remembers later feeling put out in that first Judith and then Sebastian had beaten him to the punch. Back in the bedroom and flicking on the kettle, Simon turns his attention to putting plastic coffee into a plastic cup whilst wondering if that was how they had been back then: a group of people a little like instant coffee, add water and stir. It had some flavour and would do for a while, but it wasn't the 'real thing'. Had he hoped that they would have been otherwise? In their various ways, he suspected they'd all had such ambition; but if so, the flavour had turned bitter by the end of that last summer. He likes to credit himself with being the first to predict the decline, but knows circumstance had the most significant part to play in his disillusionment. If he kids himself that he 'failed fast', it is not a claim to which the others would necessarily subscribe.

Of course, for Niamh and Sharon things hadn't petered out. Or perhaps they had. But once made kindred spirits by separate yet related events in which they were both complicit, needing a fresh start almost inevitably meant they leant on each other. However it had come about, Simon could not deny that their bond - forged as a byproduct of Sebastian's actions - had stood the test of time, and although he knew little of Sharon's later history with Malcolm, the fact that Niamh was still there at the end was surely testament to something. As the kettle rumbles towards its climax, he recalls how Judith used to joke - off-stage and presumably out of their hearing - that they must have been lesbians, closet at least. Although he never leapt to their defence, it was a theory to which he could never subscribe and which, to the best of his knowledge, no-one really gave any credence - least of all Sebastian.

If Sharon had been more inclined towards him rather than Alan, Simon can't help but wonder whether *he* might have been the one to have seen her through those dark last days. Would the house on Alberta Avenue - or anywhere else for that matter - have been jointly theirs? And under those circumstances, how might the future have looked had you been peering into it from the early summer of '86? Presumably it would have been different to his current life where he was trapped in an unexciting marriage, he and Dawn having successfully seen off two painful iterations of teenage tantrums and university angst as their offspring experienced similar rituals and adventures to those which had to some degree been liberating for him. Sharon surely wouldn't have stood for any of that nonsense. As he pours water onto the coffee granules he can't help but assess whether his children had, like him, regarded entrance into university as a means of escape. Perhaps an associated sense of freedom had burgeoned for Dawn too - though she never showed any sign that she couldn't wait for them to 'fly the nest'. Now the next phase of their joint future stretches out to a horizon which - contrary to popular belief - to him seems far from hazy. Simon is well used to the monotony of his daily and weekly routine, and can almost see nothing else ahead of him other than drudge in a desert of sameness.

He asks himself again whether it would it have been the same with Sharon. If she had accepted his advances, his proposal, would he now have found himself facing into an alternative version of a bleak future? He doubts it for two reasons. The first is that the two women were - or, with one living, is it 'are'? - very different people. He likes to think Sharon would have sparked something in him, a different Simon, one closer to the adventurer he aspired to be when he originally arrived - indeed, when he last made coffee in this very same hotel! He also wonders how such an outcome would have affected the others. Would he have been a sufficient prize and offered enough of a future to keep Sebastian at bay? And what would have happened to Alan without his two years with Sharon? Simon carries his coffee to the window and looks out, as if expecting to see Alan still waiting at the pedestrian crossing. That's an easy one, he tells himself: the answer is nothing. Nothing would have happened to Alan. Or perhaps - and this the only alternative - he might have formed a liaison with Niamh, peas from the same pod. Second prize perhaps. Or even third. But then making a meaningful connection with Niamh had seemed unlikely to all of them - except Sharon, as it turned out.

Tasting inauthentic - plastic granules, plastic milk, plastic cup - Simon submits to drinking the coffee anyway. He had made his approach to Sharon over coffee. Although he now knows it had not been the most romantic of declarations, it had been one entirely appropriate considering their situation; and hadn't Sharon seen it coming? Had he not given her clue enough throughout the latter part of '85 and into the following year? Without doubt he had made an effort, tried to be more attentive during that Spring, laid what he thought were sound enough foundations. He majored on the pragmatic and practical, told her he was sure that their coming together made perfect sense. With that being the highest card in his hand, he had no idea Sharon was holding a fistful of trumps and only needed to play a minor one to send him packing. Simon remembers her laughing, not in a malicious or malevolent way, but rather as he might have done when a younger version of Jonathan continually miscalculated the speed of his Scalextric car causing it to spin out on a tight bend. In a way Sharon had sent him spinning too. Perhaps that had been the start of something rather than its end; isn't that the better way to think about it? However, in taking up with Alan just a couple of months later, Sharon pressed the accelerator just a little harder.

§

Niamh

"I'm not surprised," she had said, looking across to where Sharon sat looking away from her, glancing out of the front room window, an empty coffee cup at her feet. They had been in Niamh's old flat where, post-Judith, the small second bedroom remained empty. Sharon had turned up out of the blue, apparently needing to divest herself of some news.

"You're not?" There had been a slightly bemused look on Sharon's face ever since she had arrived.

"Of course not!" Niamh laughed. "It's been blatantly obvious for a while that he was going to make some kind of play. You can't say you didn't notice?"

Sharon shook her head, her smile slightly wider now.

"Really?!" Niamh's incredulity made them both laugh.

"Simon?" Sharon considers the word for a moment as if it contains all the clues she needs. "No, I have to say I didn't see it coming. I'd assumed that his general good mood and bonhomie was due to factors outside of our little group; that perhaps he'd found himself a lady-friend at the office. It never occurred to me that he was trying to soften me up. Considering..."

She allowed the word to trail away.

"Considering?"

"Oh, that business with Jude. You could be forgiven for thinking he might have learned his lesson, couldn't you?"

"Oh, that." Niamh attempts to draw a parallel but fails; Sharon and Judith are animals at the opposite ends of most spectrums. "But you're so completely different. In a good way I mean."

Sharon laughs, then allows the smile to slip from her lips.

"Be careful though."

"Careful? Why?"

"Because you're probably next. I might be wrong, but..."

Having put down her book to finish the hot chocolate she habitually makes herself before bed each evening, Niamh recalls their conversation. It is a remembering which is not out of place considering they will be back together the next day - all except Sharon, of course. Over the past few days she has thought about them all on and off; recreated little historical vignettes in preparation. And although Judith, Simon, Alan and Sebastian have thus far only made cameo appearances virtually, it is Sharon who has been front and centre throughout; the pivot, the catalyst, the North Star about which they all orbited. Or at least that is Niamh's view.

Judith

She is surprised not to immediately recognise the house when she first drives along Alberta Avenue, the distraction foisted on her by the SatNav insisting she has arrived at her destination compounded by a sudden wondering how the name of a Canadian province came to be adopted for a suburban street in the south of England. Perhaps there was once a royal connection. Judith knows little about Canada having only tiptoed into it once during a visit to Niagara Falls, but she has told herself that - lured by the romance of the thing - she will return one day to take the train across the country, east to west.

Reaching the end of the road, she swings the car round at the t-junction and retraces her steps. She recalls couplets of rather drab semi-detached fifties-built houses sitting low and squat, hunkering down behind scrawny privet hedges; but much seems to have changed. She is surprised by the number of trees lining the road and is stunned to think they might have always been there and simply escaped her attention. The hedges have matured now, enhanced by the odd beech and yew; fences have been erected and repainted; and houses have been extended - upwards and sideways - so that many of them sit newly proud on their old land, heads held high. She thinks of the name again and it strikes her how the place seems closer to having earned the nomenclature 'Avenue'.

Driving slowly past, as far as she can tell number thirty-seven has not been made any larger. Its exterior has evidently been decorated sufficiently recently for it to stand out as one of the more smartly dressed residences there, and from what she can see - the trimming of the hedge, the wrought-iron gate, the lawn and flower beds beyond - it has been well-tended too. She wonders if Sharon had been the preeminent gardener, then settles on Niamh as the more likely.

Ignoring an available space almost immediately outside the house, she allows the car to roll on a little further before coming to a halt on the opposite side of the road outside number eighteen. For no other reason than to buy herself time, she compares the appearance of the two properties - Niamh and Sharon's, and this anonymous other - and confirms the former is undoubtedly superior. Even though she is someone attuned to the importance of first impressions, she is not sure what that tells her. She thinks back to the young man at Starbuck's and smiles, then glances to the passenger seat where her handbag, phone and scarf await. Luis Vuitton, Apple, Burberry: gifts rather than presents, the trappings which accompany her life. There is, she knows, a tangible financial value for such brands being seen, photographed, associated with a certain lifestyle. Image is everything. Truth be told, Judith is not a fan of Burberry; there is something a little too 'rudimentary' about some of their designs, and she was once told that, thanks to certain sport-related associations, it has suffered from some unsavoury connections. But other than to be seen at higher profile events, she cares little about sport, and any potential distaste for being linked with the retailer is more than offset by the retainer they pay her to be seen with their products.

Slipping the phone into her bag and draping the scarf about her neck, Judith then glances into the mirror secreted behind the now pulled down sun-shade. One final check. How had she looked the last time she had stepped over the threshold of number thirty-seven? She dreads to think. Had it been before or after her leaving party? And how had she left them, Sharon and Niamh: in a semi-drunken haze or with a fond farewell? In Niamh's case, Judith finds herself unconcerned; she is just about to reset their relationship, to re-engage based on the revised landscape they now inhabit. Having said that, it is not starting again exactly but rather a resumption - however brief - following a period during which the ground rules have surely changed. Her confidence is not merely based on her innate sense of superiority - on how things once were which, she is confident, will stand her in good stead today - but also in knowing she will be here for less than forty-eight hours, and how much damage can be done in two days? Soon enough she will be back in her coupé, placing her bag and watch and scarf on the seat next to her, and plugging her next destination into the navigation system. No obligation will be accompanying her unless she chooses to accept one.

What gives her pause, however, is an awareness of the myriad of sundry things over which she has limited or no control. Niamh and the others are surely open to manipulation, but the one person who might matter most in terms of how she chooses to measure herself will not be there. In Sharon's case there can be no reset, no adjustment, no correction or fresh start. Judith has to live with the legacy of how things were left, how Sharon had regarded her, how she had felt about her in the end. With a shiver, she realises she isn't entirely sure how solid those foundations might have been. Is it important? On one level, probably not; yet Judith finds herself needing to know, to understand - and in doing so, recognises that the only way she can resolve this particular conundrum is through the recollection and reportage of the rest of them. "This isn't about us, it's about Sharon" she recalls Niamh saying over the phone. It had been an assertion she'd happily accepted without quibble, but now, on the verge of once again walking through the door of number thirty-seven - of potentially even sleeping in Sharon's old bed for goodness sake! - she is not so sure. How can it not be about them?

Judith pushes up the visor and looks straight ahead. The remainder of the street unfolds before her; trees, fences, greenery and parked cars. It will be the same in two days' time. Surely everything will be the same in two days' time.

§

Alan

Giving the impression of being totally undecided, Alan's eyes scan the slim Room Service menu. He has not been drawn to it by the fare on offer, and had he been seeking dinner with above average potential he would have already dropped it back onto the windowsill and headed for the door. Not only is there an absence of imagination in the choices presented - 'Fish'n'Chips', 'Lasagne', 'Sausage with Herb Mash' - he can already imagine how such dishes will be dressed on the plate. Or not. Yet he continues to hold the menu because he has made a decision: he will suffer Room Service.

He has no doubt offerings in the restaurant downstairs will be slightly more fulsome, and whilst the staples listed before him now will also be in evidence there, he is confident they will be complemented by a few others, possibly including the ubiquitous 'Chef's Special'. Yet he has no desire to go down to the restaurant, nor bypass the in-house food altogether to seek out something else nearby, a gastro-pub perhaps, or even making the short walk into town. His reasoning is simple enough: he doesn't want to risk running into Simon. As he vacillates between 'Steak'n'Ale Pie' and 'Penne Carbonara', he is acutely aware that his reluctance is hardly rational; after all, they will be spending the best part of the next couple of days together - assuming they make the decision to reconvene on Sunday morning, an option Niamh has left open. Whether or not they do so, he will not be in a position to avoid anyone tomorrow. Yet a little like his dilly-dallying on the walk up from the station, he tells himself the secret to positive engagement is all about being mentally prepared.

Predicting that the hotel chef is least likely to bugger up the pie, that is what Alan settles on and phones down his order accordingly. "Twenty minutes" he is told. Enough time to wind up the microwave, heat things through, throw them onto a plate and then trudge them up the stairs. Or perhaps the staff have a private lift that is actually working. As he returns the menu to where he found it he notices the '£5 tray supplement' in the small print and sighs, simultaneously wondering at what level of additional charge he would have chosen to take the risk, to have gone downstairs and rushed through the lobby hoping to escape unseen.

If he thinks of Sharon at this point it is because doing so reminds him why he is there. It re-grounds him somehow, and casts the negative - like the lumpy bed, the faulty desk light, the stain on the carpet near the en suite, and, yes, even the 'tray supplement' - in a new light. None of those things matter. In a way Simon doesn't matter either. And himself too, perhaps? Returning to Niamh's assertion that they are all there for Sharon offers him a sense of balance, perhaps even of satisfaction. For the next thirty-six hours everything else should be inconsequential - the very thing that Sharon wasn't.

He has always missed her, yet now that feeling has managed to malignly expand into permanence, a solidity disqualifying even the remote possibility of the missing being circumvented by lack of courage or the discomfort of a train ride or long drive. Her death has hit him harder than he had expected. Perhaps the ache he feels bears no comparison with the pain he felt the day she told him they were finished, a pain infinitely compounded when he learned of her liaison with Sebastian so soon afterwards. Even so, looking out onto the harbour from his fourth-floor window, Alan is certain he never stopped loving her. The gap she left in his life was one he hadn't realised existed until Sharon chose to fill it, and for two precious years he was a more complete person. Yet now he is entirely cognisant that the anguish populating that void - so brutally re-exposed by her throwing him over (and for which he forgave her long ago) - has lived with him ever since, an unwanted burden, like something malignant beneath his skin for which he has been unable to medicate.

Alan wonders if that was how it had been for her with the illness which had so suddenly claimed her. He knows little in terms of the facts. Niamh had been deliberately vague (he suspects partly to protect herself), but the decline - the visible decline - had apparently been as rapid as it was unexpected. He wonders if Sharon had known for a while, doing her best to camouflage her illness until it was impossible to maintain the charade any longer. It is a notion that troubles him, partly because Sharon hadn't been the kind of person to live with falsehood or to shirk the truth or a difficult situation - wasn't he proof of that? - yet she was also the kind of friend who would resolutely try and protect those she really loved. And maybe, in the final analysis, the one person she ended up loving more than anyone - herself included - had been Niamh.

§

Sebastian

He had asked his father if he knew anyone in the hotel trade on the South Coast and had been rewarded with an introduction to Tommy and 'The Busted Flush' gastro pub. Hardly on the coast, it was nearly twenty miles from where he needed to end up, but at least it wasn't that flea-bitten excuse for a hotel with which he suspected Simon and Alan would make do. 'The Busted Flush' offered small but comfortable 'bijou' rooms, individually decorated, with a restaurant attached to the main bar offering food that had a reputation for being a cut above the average. The heavy discount Sebastian had been able to secure thanks to the familial connection contrived to make the whole package a no-brainer.

Tommy had been an old playing partner of his father's, the two of them spending three years on the same team before the latter's first international call-up catapulted one career upwards and injury sent the other's spiralling in the opposite direction. Now sliding into an ex-sportsman's all too typical physical decline, Tommy showed no signs of bitterness when Sebastian arrived, greeting him as if he were a long-lost nephew and plying him with whisky before launching into a friendly tirade against his father. The residual affection was self-evident.

"I've no idea how he got those nicknames," Tommy had smiled. "I mean, 'The Winged Wonder', 'The Stephenson Rocket'… Complete bollocks if you ask me! Your old man was never as fast as everyone made out; it was just that all the other buggers were so dreadfully slow!"

For Sebastian, such badinage was familiar. Over the years he had become used to approbation applied to his father being couched in contrary terms, and regarded such friendly complaints as something of a false positive; it is only because the charges made were blatantly untrue - and the fellow-feeling so obviously real - that they could be made at all. He recalls the ribbing his father took as soon as he retired, allowing himself to the luxury to appear to concur with his deprecators - and all in the manner of a man confident they *knew* that for a short while he had been the fastest winger in England. Having the security of one successful career behind him - as demonstrated by those international caps and various club and country records - his remodelling of himself into something of a media icon turned Hugh Stephenson into the epitome of the 'self-made man'.

Sitting in his room's compact armchair, Sebastian stares towards the turned-down Queen-sized bed accusingly, as if it is about to be responsible for something over which he has no control. Delaying his surrender to the crisp white sheets merely offers an illusion of choice; he is well aware that, no matter what time he turns out the light, it will be seven a.m. when it is seven a.m. - not a moment before or after - and that the alarm on his phone will then rouse him into the new day. If that were not the case, if he really did have some choice in the matter, then perhaps he would not be there at all, avoiding the need to endure this pre-event pantomime. Indeed, given such freedom might he have chosen to bypass the main event altogether? He glances at the empty tumbler on the small table at his side and tries to persuade himself that all of this - 'The Busted

Flush', the room, Tommy, the dinner and the drinks afterwards - is actually demonstration not of compulsion but of Free Will. He is here because he wants to be.

"Where did the name come from," he had asked Tommy, "'The Busted Flush' I mean?"

Tommy had laughed.

"It's a reminder of the past," he had said, still resolutely upbeat. "While others like your dad forged on, injury left me behind. I'd been dealt a loosing hand - as well as a busted knee. So when I cashed in my chips and decided to invest in this place, well, it seemed appropriate to reference my erstwhile career."

"But this place is a success though?" Sebastian said, instantly regretting the way he had phrased his question.

Tommy took it on the chin. He'd had a reputation as a hard man, and boasted cauliflower ears to prove it.

"It keeps me off the streets."

In the solitude and quiet of his room, the name - 'The Busted Flush' - nags at Sebastian, as if it is pertinent to him, to all of them. Over the years he has picked up snippets regarding their various adventures - and, in Judith's case, misadventures - dipping in and out with the odd enquiry, being surprised by the occasional birthday card. Wondering if it is too late for redemption - for those that require redeeming, that is - he suspects the weekend will demonstrate whether or not such miracles are possible. Were he still a betting man, he has a decent enough idea on whom he would be inclined to invest; or then again, would it make more sense to keep his money in his pocket? Of all of them, he imagines it likely that Niamh will be the most 'sorted', and that the others will all be failures in their own way. A voice - not unlike his father's - echoes the words 'The Busted Flush' and wants to know how he sees himself. Sebastian bats the voice away.

Instead he tries to focus on Sharon, the reason he is sitting where he is, staring at the beckoning sheets, contemplating what is soon to follow. It is too late for any kind of redemption in her case of course, irrespective of whether or not she would have been the least likely to require any. Even without any meaningful contact, his feelings towards her - an uneasy blend of respect and guilt - have perhaps deepened over the years, and occasionally he has found himself using his memory of her as a yardstick with which to judge others. Granted, there may be an element of the rose-tinted in his post-eighties assessment of her, but the standard she represents is one of the few things not to have let him down in the intervening years. Respect and guilt, yes, but there is a modicum of duty there too and it is the latter which motivates him now.

On the drive down from Manchester (where he had been in the audience for his father's annual appearance on the "Veteran's Special" edition of 'A Question of Sport') he had speculated as to what his attitude to the weekend might have been if the reunion were something other than a wake, if Sharon had not been dead. Perhaps he would have been stirred sufficiently to consider rekindling something of the old Sebastian. Yes, he had been a mess towards the end of their time together, but surely it was not too much of a stretch to concoct a scenario - and a persona - which saw the arrival of a mature, revitalised and dashing Sebastian, one as irresistible now as he had felt back then. And surely he *had* been irresistible. Wasn't the evidence incontrovertible? But if he had been on the M6 in transit to a re-run, where - as a Lothario in his mid-fifties - would he have focussed his attention? Not on Sharon. No matter how he felt about her back then, his respect for her having grown in absentia, he gifted himself with sufficient credit to assume he wouldn't risk tarnishing that - though had he been similarly inclined to recall his precise attitude towards her during the summer of '88, he would surely have found himself embarrassed. Running through his hypothesis again and continuing to avoid the lure of a soft mattress, Sebastian again arrives at the same answer as he had once he had broken out from the stranglehold of the motorway:

Judith. If he is not quite as invincible now as he had been all those years ago, from what he can tell Judith was similarly demonstrating all the signs of being an increasingly less formidable woman. Given she was not the force of old, how could she not be vulnerable to him once again? On that basis, just how far from his peak did he actually need to be in order to resurrect something with her?

There had been nothing remarkable in the young and naïve version of himself being seduced by her beauty. Who hadn't been? In his case, however, he is cognisant of there having been something very reciprocal. In the same way as she stood out above everyone, so metaphorically he towered head and shoulders over Simon and Alan. Hardly competition. And surely that must still be the case. It would not have taken a genius to calculate that at some point he and Judith would spark off each other, drawn inexorably into collisions which were to provide the backing track to their lives for over three years. That they egged each other on was, he knows, undeniable. In an instant Judith would suddenly effervesce and he would be lost, after which they would fuse for a short while until the tension became too great for one or other of them. Like magnets of the same polarity, they were suddenly forced apart - only for him to do something exceptional which would spin her around and lure her back in. Or, on occasion, vice versa. And so the cycle would begin again. Sebastian remembers the excitement and the passion, the thrill of the chase, the depth of rage and anger, the moments of pure tenderness. Although they never spoke of it, he suspects they both knew there could be no future in their compulsive crashing together. It was as if - when they were on the rebound from each other - the only person they could possibly rebound to was the person from whom they had just broken; a virtuous - and virtue-less - circle, emotion on a sine wave. Consciously planned or otherwise, eventually he found a way to fracture the cycle, though sitting here in 'The Busted Flush' at what cost he did so he remains unable to calculate. Had it saved or destroyed him? And the others? There were inevitable ripples, after all. Were the shockwaves from his actions the catalyst for Judith's abandonment? Perhaps she was already on the verge of leaving. Yet even though that is the narrative to which she has always adhered, Sebastian is certain he gave her a hefty shove at an opportune moment - or an inopportune one, depending on your perspective.

Charm had been his trump card back then. He had been smothered in it growing up, feeding on it as it radiated from a father who was simply 'a natural'. Very early on Sebastian had learned how to get his way - not with the elder Stephenson who knew all the tricks of the trade - but with his mother, then later from his friends and Masters at the Public School he attended. Godwinson's had prepared him perfectly for University; supremely self-confident, he still believes he could have taken any subject and charmed his way through it. Oh, he built up a reputation as something of a rogue of course, but wasn't that what university was all about, finding yourself, making the most of it? It was this boyish allure which hooked Judith, and then later - and very briefly - Niamh too. And though, between the two of them, he tells himself Sharon had fallen under his spell in the same way, he finds the argument less convincing; there was something else in play, something over which she rather than he had control. Perhaps it was that notion which fostered his subsequent respect for her.

Not that he regards his entanglement with Sharon as a failure in any way. But subsequently there *had* been failures; women who were either too hardened by life - or too wise - to be taken in by him. Under such circumstances he would simply move on. That he had chosen not to do so with Melissa can only be regarded as the biggest mistake of his life - or the only mistake that mattered. She had succumbed to his charm of course, and there had been something about her which enveloped him in fashion that no-one since Judith had managed. In her own way, Melissa had been exceptional; not quite as beautiful as Judith nor quite as intelligent, yet she still presented something of a challenge to him. Yes, her father was a friend of his own; and yes, her family had been exceptionally wealthy; and yes, he had been on the rebound from a somewhat disastrous encounter with a married Italian faux-countess; and yes, he had been under pressure from his mother to 'settle down'. All in all, a cocktail that perhaps inevitably subsumed him. Deciding that Melissa represented the entirely of his future, Sebastian placed all his chips on her and spun the wheel. Needing the ball to fall into red, when it eventually landed in black he pursued the only course open to him: he started finding fault, blaming her for just about anything he could think of. Even though he didn't really want children, the fact that they had none was down to her; being overlooked for promotion at work was a result of the domestic demands she placed on him; and when their respective fathers fell out over a dubious investment proposed by Melissa's, the die was cast.

But all that now feels like ancient history. With a sigh of resignation, he stands, checks the curtains are closed, and beings to undress. He is booked in for a second night, though has no real idea what to expect from tomorrow evening. It is possible that the meal - indeed, the day as a whole - will be a disaster; if that proves to be the case, then an early escape is all he can hope for. Alternatively, he might be so positively absorbed in their reconnection that he ends up too drunk to drive in which case his unarticulated backup plan is a sofa at Niamh's. He remembers that Judith is staying there, and - glancing again at the bed - wonders if there might yet be a more comfortable and rewarding outcome than having to resort to a blanket thrown over him in a cold living room. Walking into the en-suite, he regards himself in the mirror, searching for some residue of that irresistible charm. Perhaps now undermined by well-worn skin and a few wrinkles, if he still has it - or enough of it, at least - then it will be in his eyes. Windows of the soul? He wouldn't go that far.

Gathering

Niamh & Alan

"How was dinner last night?"

Having walked on ahead of the others, they are a few yards into the cemetery when Niamh breaks the silence.

"Dinner?"

"I assume you had dinner with Simon; you each knew the other was staying in the same hotel."

"Ah." Alan looks around as they walk, noting how many of the crosses have been laid down onto the graves themselves. Once, when he had queried the practice, Sharon told him that's what they did if the stones became unstable, to protect relatives and visitors. "We didn't actually meet until this morning at breakfast. We arrived at different times last night and were probably both tired; I know I was." He is conscious of the white lie, then expands the untruth. "Having said that, I half expected to get a call from him."

"And at breakfast, how was it? After so long, I mean."

Alan glances at Niamh.

"Honestly?"

"Of course."

He catches a trace of her smile before looking ahead to where the path forks.

"I think it was a shade uncomfortable for both of us."

"Even after all this time?"

"Well, it wasn't exactly great when we last met, was it?" Alan delivers the sentence as if it were a reminder of an event at which she had been present. "And in the interim… Well, time passes. Life, you know? I think it's fair to say that neither of us did very much in the way of remediation - if that's the right word."

"None of us have been very good at that, keeping in touch." Unconcerned about searching for the mot juste, she leads him to the left, glancing over her shoulder to check the others are not too far behind. "I suspect there will be a fair bit of that today; awkwardness. I think that's one reason why Sharon wanted us to do this; to see if we could get over all those obstacles from the past, to get over ourselves."

"I confess I'm a little surprised she actually believed we'd all turn up, never mind how we might find it - as an experience, I mean. Do you think she knew it would be difficult?" Alan asked.

"I'm not sure." Niamh thinks for a second. "Probably - though that wouldn't have disqualified doing it, not in her mind. Perhaps she wanted to give us the chance to try and retrieve something she thought we'd lost - whether we realised it or not - both individually and as a group. Or to shut some doors for good maybe, if you accept some might still be ajar."

"After all this time?"

"Although she never said as much, towards the end I'm guessing she spent a lot of time thinking back to the old days and to what we'd had back then - and she knew she was never going to have a chance to make amends, if amends needed to be made. You could see her request as a kind of gift if you wanted to."

"That sounds like Sharon."

"Does it?" Niamh looks away. Off to her left an elderly couple are standing by a grave; the man - one arm about the woman - holds some withered flowers in his free hand. Niamh hated to see flowers gone over like that. Who are they remembering: brother or sister, son or daughter? Niamh wonders if this weekend will see the execution of some kind of ritual for the five of them too. Or for her at least. Alan's words - "That sounds like Sharon" - strike her as odd; how can he have known *her* Sharon, the woman she had become after the rest of them had walked away? Only she had witnessed the growth, the changes, the highs and lows; only she knew the final incarnation of the person to whom they were now paying tribute. Perhaps part of the reason Sharon had wanted them to come back was to reintroduce herself, for them to understand what had become of her. If that was the case, then the burden for that task fell squarely on Niamh's shoulders.

But she doesn't blame Alan for his assertion. His comment is based on how he has chosen to remember her, a memory he has nurtured across the intervening years. It will surely be the same for all of them. If they left with a single composite image of Sharon as she had been at the end of the eighties, then they will have returned with five subtly different appreciations of her now, their individual snapshots corrupted by time, by superficial knowledge of her history and her illness, and by their own lives. She knows Alan's assessment is likely to be the most valid because - with the exception of herself - he had been the most intimate with Sharon for the longest period; that, and because it would have been in his nature to try and preserve the truth of her, wanting his fondest memories to remain unadulterated for as long as possible. Such simple honesty is one of the traits she admires most in him; it is a characteristic she likes to believe she also sees echoed in herself. For some women such simplicity might be attractive, a magnet of sorts, yet she had never harboured any romantic feelings towards him; during the short taxi ride from her house to the cemetery, and now as they walk on together, she is acutely aware that she still does not. Reconciling her assessment of Alan with the feelings Sharon once had for him is an activity Niamh is not inclined to undertake at present; rather she is grateful that one of this weekend's reconnections should be so straightforward.

Even though she has already spent longer with Judith than anyone else - the simple dinner, an evening in front of the television - Niamh has yet to crystallise what she makes of her jet-setting friend. She had arrived flamboyantly, wafted into the house as if she had recently appeared on a chat show and had yet to put her public persona to bed - all of which left Niamh unable to pin down exactly who Judith had become. Much about her seemed to be merely surface-deep, and even a glass or two of wine failed to break through that particular veneer. Niamh concludes that if uncertainty arose from the previous evening's encounter then it was only to be expected, so forgives herself for not being able to resolve that particular equation - something which only supplements her gratitude to Alan for being so straightforward.

She slips her arm through his.

"Not far now," she says.

It is a gesture which brings Alan comfort rather than any frisson of excitement. Having previously come to regard Niamh as the sister he never had, there is something reassuring in feeling her arm through his, and in a way he is elevated by her gesture, as if it is a statement of trust. Looking back he sees the other three meandering after them. Although their two taxis had arrived at the same time, both Judith and Sebastian had been somewhat slow when disembarking, a delay compounded by Simon arresting them at the gates and pointing to something on the other side of the road where the land sloped steeply downwards and through the municipal gardens to meet the promenade, the beach, the sea. It is, Alan thinks, fitting that he had shared a cab with Niamh, and that they were walking on together. Of the five of them, surely they were the two who had the most meaningful connection to their departed friend.

Niamh leads him away from the path and through rows of headstones which are more densely congregated than those they had already passed. At the base of some, urns rested alongside vases and pots; in one or two places, small bushes - box, hebe, fuchsia - had been planted as a permanent tribute, or to avoid any compulsion for a constant return with new flowers. Alan notes that where there are flowers in some cases the blooms are fresh and vibrant; in others, all that remain are a few withered stems. He thinks back to the elderly couple he saw earlier.

Forced to a halt, Alan looks down. Sharon's headstone is modest, adorned with just her name and two dates: 1962 and 2018. There is no further inscription, no vase, no flowers.

"She wanted it to be as simple as possible," Niamh says, as if she can read his mind. "I tried to persuade her otherwise, but she was adamant. 'There's no point', I remember her saying. 'If I'm not going to live on - which I'm not - then a slab of marble's not going to make the slightest difference.'" Niamh offers a small laugh. "She never said the difference between what though."

What she doesn't tell Alan is how often she has been here since Sharon died, nor how, having been unable to stop the tears for days afterwards, she feels all cried out. She doesn't tell him how she had been here just two days previously and quietly asked Sharon what she wanted her to do with them all, what she expected from the weekend. Had she done so, then she'd also have to tell him that her question had gone unanswered.

"It must have been really difficult at the end," Alan says - then adds, "For both of you, I mean."

"Me?" Niamh contemplates how profoundly weak a word like 'difficult' is. "It was tough, of course - yet infinitely harder after she'd gone."

More from instinct than anything else, Alan wants to ask another question but is unsure what is appropriate - and even if he knew, he doubts he would be able to find the words. Suddenly conscious of the others approaching, he is relieved of his obligation.

"She hated it," Niamh goes on, as if she has been waiting for them to gather, for all movement to stop. "Being ill, I mean. I'm not sure how long she'd known or had an inkling; she never said. But once it became obvious and diagnosed, well... It was as if, being acknowledged and out in the open, her sickness was suddenly free to take over. Perhaps that's how things are." She pauses, not to allow the others to speak - they do not - but simply to gather her thoughts. "I think it was the indignity of it that upset her most. That and being powerless to do anything about it. It's strange. I always thought she was a fighter - you may remember her as a fighter, I don't know - but it was as if she caved in, not wanting to prolong the inevitable. There was almost a sense of 'let's get this over with then' about her. Maybe it was born from a desire not to cause a fuss: for the hospital, for me, for herself even. When she was experiencing one of her frequent low points she'd get angry. And she'd swear like a trooper. That was one of the ways she'd let it out. Sometimes the episodes were funny, those tirades of hers; so loud and foul-mouthed. Even in the hospital. Used to make me laugh - which then made her laugh too, probably at the ridiculousness of it all." She hears a soft smothered chuckle behind her and tries to place it without looking round. Sebastian probably; and maybe Judith too, she isn't sure. "But then, in an instant, it was all over, intrusion kept to a minimum. Small service, small congregation, small headstone. Which is obtuse really, when you think how Sharon wasn't a 'small' person… I don't think she was small to any of us. And this - " she gestures to the marble with a small movement of her foot, "this isn't her. It isn't even a means of remembering her. Not really. I think that's another of the reasons she wanted us all here, together again. We're all that's left of her life now."

And then Niamh surprises herself by finding she can cry one more time.

§

Niamh & Judith

"Do you remember those few months I lived with you?"

Judith had hung back as the others drifted away, knowing Niamh would be the last to leave Sharon.

Niamh glances up at her, surprised more by the question than the slightly false accent in which it is delivered. Judith sounds as if she is in a rehearsal for something.

"How could I not?"

"And then we hooked up with Sharon. The three of us." Judith pauses as if her statement is sufficient to encompass a lifetime's worth of experience. She looks at Niamh cocooned in her oh-so-practical coat, waiting for a signal of some kind. "For a while I wanted us to be female Musketeers."

They start walking after the others and back toward the cemetery entrance. Rather than get a taxi to return to Niamh's, they have agreed to walk through the municipal gardens, down to the promenade, and then stop for coffee at what used to be 'Gino's' Ice Cream Parlour. Revisiting the fabric of an old haunt seemed to have found a degree of universal appeal. After that they would separate for a while - Judith and Niamh to Alberta Avenue, Simon and Alan returning to the hotel - and then reconvene at the restaurant. No-one knew precisely what Sebastian's plans were, not even Niamh. With Judith secured and in step, Niamh can't help but notice the spaces between the men walking ahead of them, distances too great to suggest any meaningful conversation is taking place. Judith's voice brings her back.

"We were so young then, weren't we? Young and naïve. Embarking on something we didn't yet understand."

"You and I for sure," Niamh agrees, "though don't forget Sharon was just that little bit older."

"And in some ways already settled, I suppose." Judith pauses. "It's been quite a journey." She nods towards the men walking ahead. "For some more than others."

Niamh, unsure what to make of the comment or who it is aimed at, lets it go. Judith is right about the journey, of course, and how far they have come since then - but in what terms? Probably not all of them have advanced as much as they might have - and almost certainly not her. Convinced they no longer compete on the same level playing field as they once had, she struggles to recall just how 'equal' they had been all those years ago - for even now she likes to assume they must have been so.

"Do you remember that time we went to the funfair?"

Judith laughs in response.

"God, yes! Whose idea had that been? I can't remember. I've got the feeling we were still hungover from the night before, which must have helped make the long drive seem like a good idea."

"I definitely was," Niamh confesses with a smile. "I threw up as soon as I got off the Waltzer!"

"We should never have gone on that thing. It was crazy! Just shows you though."

"What?"

"Oh, I don't know." Judith allows her modern-day self to catch up with the younger incarnation she had been back then, concocting the image of a person she simultaneously misses yet is glad has gone. "I think we were trying to impress the boys. Wasn't that what we did then?" Half a beat. "And you…"

"What about me?" Niamh asks, her mind still dredging up images from that day, the awfulness of the drive home, how ill she had subsequently felt.

"Well it wasn't really like you, was it? The funfair, I mean. Neither you nor Sharon tended to let your hair down as much as the rest of us."

Niamh laughs again.

"No-one let their hair down as much as you and Seb, though the other boys tried in a half-hearted, amateurish way. Things like the

Waltzer were the sorts of experience Sharon tended to steer clear of."

"She was very - picky," Judith suggests, though without conviction.

"What do you mean?"

"Only that she knew when to have fun and when not; when to join in; how much to drink or how far to go. She was better at calculating than the rest of us." Judith pauses. "At least most of the time."

"All of that stuff... I was out of my depth."

"Meaning?"

Reaching the main gate, they have paused to check the traffic before crossing the road and walking into the park. From their right come the sounds of tennis balls being pinged backwards and forwards over nets, and, beyond the courts, cries of children in the playground. Niamh tries to recall if she'd ever enjoyed herself like that when she had been a child.

"My upbringing, I suppose," she says, picking up the thread. "Although I've always lived in England, my parents moved over from County Cork before I was born - separately, of course. They met and married here. But they were still tied to Ireland, to their own parents; people you might have characterised as simple, God-fearing folk. They were mainly rural, country types, living off the land. Dublin was the evil big city - at least for my Nana Grace - and some of what they believed and how they lived their lives inevitably rubbed off on my folks and thus, I suppose, on me and Siobhan."

"Siobhan?"

"My sister. You knew I had a sister?"

Judith smiles as if to assure Niamh she did - then suddenly realises not only that she did not, but that she actually knows very little about any of them. Except Sebastian. Does her lack of knowledge cause her to feel guilty? She parks the question.

"I'm sure you must have told me."

"So anyway, a trip to the funfair, boys, drinking? There was a large part of me - embedded in my DNA if you like - for which all such adventures were foreign. We'd grown up, Siobhan and I, enjoying ourselves in different ways; ways that I'm sure most people would have found boring. And university didn't cure me of my reserve, if that's what you'd call it. Nor Siobhan's. She went back to Ireland soon after she graduated."

"When did you last see her?"

"A year or so ago, I suppose. Sharon and I went over for a long weekend. It was - I don't know - unsettling somehow. Though mostly for who I've no idea."

They reach a circular paved area in the middle of which a fountain is located. Two families are perched on its edge holding on to small children who are trying to spot any fish that might be swimming in the reservoir which feeds the fountain. Each child appears as an uneven reflection of itself with the rippling water acting as mirror. On the other side of the pond three paths branch off, each eventually leading down to the promenade; at various points on the way down, spurs join the paths together and allow walkers to adopt meandering zig-zag routes. Judith and Niamh pause.

"I wonder which one they took?" Judith looks to each in turn, searching for a glimpse of a head, a coat, something she recognises. As she does so, she realises the park is one of the few things that time seems not to have changed.

Rather than assist in the somewhat perfunctory search, Niamh watches Judith. Even in her mid-fifties she is stunning, and Niamh is reminded of one of the major facets in the gulf between the two of them. There is an elegance in the way Judith stands, a practiced perfection in how she lifts her hand to shade her eyes. To all intents and purposes, she seems to be a person who - consciously or otherwise - knows she is on display and revels in the role.

"Is that why you left?" Niamh asks as soon as Judith has spotted their companions and started toward the central of the three paths.

"Left?"

"Moved out from that awful flat of mine in Parham Road. Was I - I don't know - too 'provincial' for you?"

Judith glances at her and tries, in that instant, to see whether or not she can map Niamh's journey from Parham Road to here and now, thirty years later, walking again through the municipal gardens; not mapping it in terms of what she has done or experienced, but rather in how she has grown and how she has changed. Or not.

"I enjoyed those few months," she offers, skirting the question, "even if the flat was pretty dreadful! You gave me a solid platform in a new and unfamiliar place. You and Sharon, of course. I don't think I could have wished for a better start."

"But?"

"Is there always a 'but'?"

"Pretty much," Niamh says.

Judith smiles.

"I realised I needed my own space, I suppose. I didn't know what I wanted back then - did any of us? - and I found I had to have an environment in which I could make discoveries and mistakes without impinging on anyone else. And I think I must have been something of a slob, so you were probably glad to see me go. I've never been particularly domesticated. Unlike you and Sharon." She allows her statement to float away across the herbaceous borders.

"'It's not you, it's me'; isn't that what they say?"

"Something like that." They share a brief laugh before Judith continues. "I don't think I fitted in, to be honest."

"In what sense? You're right, you were no domestic goddess, but none of us were perfect. I didn't mind a little clearing up after you from time to time."

"You make me sound like a puppy!" Judith smiles, allowing her hand to stretch out to Niamh's arm, a gesture intended to assure Niamh she is making a joke, that there is nothing to be forgiven, no offence has been taken. For her part, Niamh knows on whose side the greater burden of responsibility for forgiveness lay.

"I don't think we made that bad a fist of it," Niamh suggests. "Once we'd settled down there was a kind of routine."

"Maybe that was the issue. I discovered I wasn't very good at routine. If there's one thing my subsequent life has demonstrated it's surely that!" She laughs, more to herself this time, and then pushes on to stop Niamh opening the door she has just left ajar. "That was territory where you and Sharon were always so much more comfortable; and even though she wasn't living with us, it soon became clear that the two of you were the most alike. At times I felt something of a gooseberry."

"Really?" Niamh remembers the occasional night out when they simply couldn't keep up with Judith; she would drive them on, force them into social situations way outside their comfort zone. The day at the funfair makes an unwelcome return. "And sometimes *we* felt like gooseberries too!"

It was the trigger for another laugh.

As the path swung to the left, dipping down slightly, the sea came fully into view. Niamh had come to judge the mood of a day by the water, its colour, the size of the waves, the sound they made on the shingle, flinging it upwards then sucking it back. They were still too high up to hear that, but the seagulls' cawing had become noticeable. It was a vista of which she and Sharon never tired.

There was a location on one of the other paths where, at the crown of a turn, a bench had been strategically placed to allow its occupants to take in the panorama. It was one of their favourite spots; yet even so, Niamh had deliberately avoided it since Sharon had died, afraid that if she sat on the bench one more time she might never be able to get up.

"I don't think Sharon ever quite understood you." Niamh edges into the calm that has manifested between them; offers up something that she has wanted Judith to know for a long time. She has done so partly because she is speaking for herself, but also because she wants to do as much as she can to square Sharon away with each of them. Yes, the weekend is about paying their respects and remembering their friend, but Niamh also thinks it has to be about drawing lines, dotting i's and crossing t's. If there are unsaid truths - or unheard ones come to that - then surely this is the time; there will not be another.

"Really?" Judith is clearly surprised, but not unpleasantly so. She has always assumed they had been transparent and uncomplicated in their own way, at least to the extent of what they were comfortable sharing; little remained secret when it came to Alan or Simon or Sebastian - though there were layers to Sebastian to which she alone had been privy. Though Judith includes herself in her assessment of their mutual transparency, the thought that there had been something of *her* which had remained a mystery to the rest of the them gives her a fillip; the notion that she might be more complex than they initially perceived is reassuring. "In what way?" she asks.

"I don't know. Perhaps she didn't understand how anyone could live their life the way you did." Niamh pauses. "Or maybe that's not quite fair; it probably has more to do with the Judith you became after you left us, the way your life changed and how that changed you."

"Or vice versa?" Judith suggests.

Niamh smiles.

"And I think she never quite got over the annoyance of your assuming that she was a lesbian, that we were a couple. Even after all the evidence of that last summer."

"But you *were* a couple," Judith insists, deliberately not picking up the sexual reference. "The two of you were more a couple than almost anyone I've ever met."

"But not like that. Never like that." Niamh searches for evidence. "I know I'm not. I *know* I'm not. And as for Sharon… What about Alan? Malcolm?" She wants to add Sebastian to her brief list but refrains from doing so. That would be cruel, and Niamh has no wish to be cruel.

Choosing not to reply, Judith sees the three men waiting a little way ahead of them. She stops walking and, shielding her eyes against a sun that has retreated behind a cloud, makes to look out to sea, to take in the view. Wanting to allow her a moment to herself, Niamh continues walking, offering a brief wave to the now stationary triumvirate.

Niamh is not wrong; Judith knows that. She had assumed the two of them had been a couple in the fullest and frankest sense of the word - and if not whilst she had still been living in and around the town, that they would soon be so. Given that last summer had been an aberration, Judith is inclined to disqualify it as the basis for conclusive evidence about anything. If one were to accept outliers such as that, who knows where you might end up in the assessment of things - especially people. Lesbian or not, Judith regards her own relationship with Sharon as somehow neutral. As she had driven south she had inevitably given Sharon a great deal of thought, examined incidents from their relatively brief shared existence; wasn't four years or so out of a total of over fifty a relatively modest percentage? And as such, can she not assign it slightly less weight than others might choose to? The inevitable byproduct of her mulling over those episodes was that she had exercised considerable brainpower in relocating all of them in her consciousness, trying to recall the concrete in order to fix them, somehow attach them to various anchor points so that she could work on them. The trip to the funfair would have been such a stake in the ground had she remembered it.

Judith, in looking out over the promenade, the beach, and down to the water, is also reminded of a sense of place - topping-up the scrapbook of memories which had re-opened as soon as she saw that road sign after the motorway. Her conclusion in all of this is to confirm, unsurprisingly, that she is not here because of *where* they are. The town, the coast, the overall scene is inconsequential - after all, she has more picturesque memories to which she can cling should necessity arise. How can this scruffy, second-rate place compare with Lerici, for example? Or Capri? At this moment the more surprising realisation is that she is not really here for Sharon either. Not at all. What Niamh had said during their conversation has only confirmed what Judith already knew, namely that she and Sharon were different to her, that she was more of an outsider in the world they inhabited so comfortably. And she knows if she can say that about Niamh and Sharon, then the same has to be true of Alan and Simon. There she has even less attachment, an indifference which is off the scale. Not even Simon's ham-fisted attempt to woo her that one time gains him any kudos at all. Thus she can only be there for Sebastian - and for herself.

Perhaps they are one and the same, two sides of the same coin. It is a notion which unsettles her. She needs to confirm that the Judith she has become is validated; that the life she has constructed for herself not only holds water, but is a cut above her old friends' lives. Having always regarded herself as 'top dog', it is a position she is keen to re-establish. Niamh, Alan and Simon represent little in the way of challenge. But against Sebastian? Perhaps in some way he is the most accurate measure of her superiority, her litmus test.

§

Judith & Simon

If one choses not to follow the gentle wheelchair-friendly slope as it winds the final few yards down to the promenade, the walker is offered the alternative of a narrow flight of steep steps to reach sea-level. It is on the penultimate one of these that Judith loses her footing, her toppling face-first onto the waiting concrete only prevented by Simon who - happening to have paused just beyond the final tread - is able to grab her upper arm and keep her sufficiently upright.

"Thank you!" she says, suddenly breathless.

"They were never particularly even, those last few," Simon replies, offering blame and exoneration in equal measure.

Freeing herself from him, equilibrium reestablished, Judith moves on, following in the footsteps of the others who have already gained twenty yards on them. As Simon falls in step, she assumes that, owing to a motive as yet undisclosed, he has been waiting for her, and if so his presence certainly proved propitious. But she is mistaken in her assumption. Indeed, Simon had been unaware just how close Judith had been to reaching sea-level until, in that single instant, he happened to catch a glimpse of her coat out of the corner of his eye and heard the beginnings of a cry. His subsequent actions had merely been instinctive.

In something of a carbon copy of Judith's detachment from Niamh earlier (that pause to admire the view), Simon, having gained the promenade, had stopped to look out to sea and watch two tankers as they slowly passed each other on the horizon, from this distance the ships seemingly within a whisker of each other yet probably separated by half a mile at least. His motivation had not been in the looking but in not moving, to provide some distance between himself and the rest, to allow Niamh to take up the baton with Alan and Sebastian. The walk down from the cemetery had been slightly strained. Whether this had been due to their reflecting on Sharon's passing or because being in each other's company was an uncomfortable experience he couldn't be sure. He suspected the latter. They had exchanged a few words and tried to find triggers teased from their shared history in order to resurrect something of that old camaraderie; once or twice a joke had been made, or a sentence started with the phrase 'Do you remember'. And in the main they did remember, though it was soon proven that memory alone was an insufficient catalyst to re-establish the amity of the old days. Was this failure simply because it was too early in their coming back together for such a gambit to be successful, or was there too much history to overcome? Had they each changed to such an extent that they were radically different people these days? Simon knows all such factors are in play, and to differing extents depending on who you considered to be populating the two sides of the equation: the point of balance (or imbalance) between he and Alan would be significantly different to that between himself and Sebastian. And now he found himself alongside Judith. An entirely different prospect.

He had been struck by her as soon as they had come together at Niamh's, that brief period of coffee and bonhomie where they exchanged the superficial while waiting for the taxis that were to take them to the cemetery. Though he knew nothing of fashion - and perhaps only a little more about women - Judith had looked stunning in what Simon took to be a calculated but understated way. She was certainly several degrees removed from the last few times he had seen her in the tabloids, or that rather gaudy travel piece in 'Hello' a few years previously when she had been running around with the now ex-racing driver whose name he could never remember. And in seeing her, he had slipped inadvertently into comparison mode, not just between today's Judith and those semi-recent images of her, but between Judith and Sharon, Judith and Niamh. And yes, even between Judith and Dawn. But in all such battles - especially any involving his wife - there could only be one winner; confirmation - if confirmation were needed - as to what he had seen in her all those years ago, and explanation enough as to why he had aspired to impossible heights, albeit briefly.

"She should have told us to bring flowers," he suggests, feeling the need to break the ice. They could hardly walk all the way to 'Gino's' in silence, and he has no desire to quicken his pace in order to reattach himself to the others.

"Do you think so?" she replies. "It was a sad, naked little plot wasn't it? Not much to show for a life."

"Simple. That's what Niamh said Sharon had wanted, so that's what she's ended up with - not that it will concern her now." A pause because he feels obliged to insert one. "Still. Flowers might have been nice."

As far as Judith can tell there is nothing romantic in his opinion; rather, he is giving her the distinct impression that his preference would be to comply with a direct instruction, as if relying on his own initiative in such matters could never deliver a suitable outcome. Is she surprised? She recalls the old Simon, the one who had approached her late that night full of his well-rehearsed declaration. The memory of the event still makes her shiver. There was nothing romantic about that either; his proposal had been based more on pragmatism than passion, on logic rather than some flavour of wild abandon - not that it would have made any difference had it been. But at least she can, in retrospect, credit him with the imagination required to even contemplate their potential liaison, however ridiculous the prospect. Did Simon's need to be told to bring flowers rather than deciding to do so off his own back in any way confirm the man he had become, like the Simon she had known then only more so? Snippets about his life - indeed, about both his and Alan's lives - have reached her sporadically over the years, usually in the occasional missive from Sharon or an impromptu email from Niamh. From what she can tell the two of them have slipped inexorably into the mundane, accepting their roles in society without question and trying to execute them to some misunderstood level of perfection. At least the fact that Alan has - by choice or otherwise - remained single ever since the end of his affair with Sharon bestows a little something to pique one's interest about him.

"Does it seem very different to you?" she asks, changing tack to safer territory.

"What?"

"This place." She waves an arm in the general direction of the town though the majority of the gesture ends up encompassing only the sea. "I spotted a few things that had changed when I was driving in; you know, a new housing estate or office building here, an industrial building missing there. I even found a drive-thru Starbucks!"

As far as Simon is concerned, her final example seems a frivolous way to measure something; hardly the Rise and Fall of the Roman Empire.

"Not that I've noticed," he says. "They haven't fixed those steps for a start!" It is intended to be a joke - but one which merely elicits a modest smile. "The ferry boats look pretty much the same as they always did - though I'm sure they must have upgraded them - and I didn't see anything out of the ordinary as we drove through the High Street; just the predictable rotation of the usual shops and brands. Even the hotel over the other side of the water is as crap today as it was way back." Judith says nothing. "You didn't stay there when you first arrived, did you?"

"No. The bank set me up in this really nice B&B a little way out of town. I was there for a couple of weeks until I found Niamh - not that her flat was a necessarily step in the right direction!"

"I vaguely remember it I think."

"Parham Road?"

"That's it." Simon recalibrates. "But you weren't there long, were you?"

Judith shakes her head, glad to be on more comfortable terrain.

"A couple of months. I moved into my flat, remember? On the top floor of that new development. Well, it was new then. Afterwards, Niamh found that little house not far from here and I think she stayed there until she and Sharon moved to Alberta Avenue together. But that was after I'd left."

"After we'd all left," Simon confirms, keen to ensure he inserts himself into the history. "I remember Niamh's house, and your flat - not that I was there very often."

In an instant Judith finds herself dragged back to the evening of Simon's declaration and wonders if that's where any conversation with him will inexorably take her. Perhaps that is the nature of history, or of relationships; like water, maybe history finds a level, some datum point where its participants are forced to wrestle with a bizarre kind of equality. If so, what will that mean for the rest of the day, particularly a day that includes Sebastian?

§

Alan & Simon

"Well this place has certainly changed."

No longer the ice cream parlour they once knew, 'Gino's' has become 'Franco's', transformed into what aspires to be an up-market coffee house. Whether or not the transformation has been entirely successful is open to both debate and personal taste. The gaudy brashness of 'Gino's' - all primary colours and formica tables - has been replaced by subtle if not sombre hues, yet for many 'Franco's' remains unlikely to hit the mark; it feels a little like the runt of the coffee chain litter. Not that Alan is surprised. Based on the time he spent in the town - as well as the odd excursion to similar places subsequently - he has settled on a theory that 'the seaside' has a way of dragging its environment down to a base level above which it is impossible to rise. Perhaps this being tethered to a lowest common denominator is due to the sand and grit which seems to get everywhere; or the clientele who, having settled on a seaside holiday (maybe for the umpteenth time!), are determined to have their expectations met, expectations which - when filled with beach balls, candy floss, and fish and chips - impose a template on just about everywhere they land. Yet amid the remodelled surfaces there is something which strikes Alan as being suspiciously the same: not exactly time-warped across thirty years, there is a certain familiarity about the staff. It is not simply the ubiquitous black-and-white uniforms nor the rather off-hand manner in which patrons are served, but - in the faces of one or two of them at least - some of the employees look exactly the same as they did when their forebears were serving '99s' topped with raspberry sauce. His unscientific conclusion is that 'Franco' is probably related to 'Gino', the next generation of the same family attempting to move their business along with the times.

Sitting across the small square table from him, Simon is looking about the place in order to conjure a suitable response to Alan's statement. When they arrived en masse they found all the larger tables taken and had to settle for a four and a two. As soon as Niamh, Judith and Sebastian grabbed the four, Alan - next through the door - had been left with no choice at all; he could hardly leave Simon on his own. As Alan waits he can hear the other three chattering just behind him, a remark from Sebastian bringing a laugh from Niamh and Judith which further echoes like a distorted flashback to the eighties.

"Dreadful place," comes Simon's considered opinion. "The decor's shabby and the tables are too close, rammed together to get as many people in as possible. I swear if I get up too quickly I'll set the next few tables toppling like dominoes." He pauses. "And I expect the coffee will be weak and bitter, too. The worst combination possible."

Alan is unable to disagree, yet he refrains from immediate comment, not wishing to perpetuate a pointless and frivolous dialogue. Indeed, he has more weighty things on his mind. Not having slept particularly well, he eventually awoke to find himself perturbed by his reaction to their arrival the previous day - particularly his insistence in avoiding Simon until it was impossible to do so any longer. Why had that been? He had travelled south knowing there were bridges to be built and that the weekend would provide him with a unique opportunity to do so. Not so much with Judith and Sebastian - and certainly not with Niamh! - but with Simon who, once upon a time, had been his best friend. Alan doesn't desire a rekindling to that kind of level - they have both moved on after all - but he feels there could be unnameable benefits in laying a few old ghosts to rest: their last meeting in London for example, or the spectre of Sharon. He told himself execution against such a plan would be a benefit to them both, yet as he sits here now, looking across the table at his erstwhile friend, there is greater proportion of stranger in his companion than he could ever have imagined possible.

Perhaps he could choose to argue that on one level such a revised starting point - a certain distance between them - might make things easier; yet their history is not soluble, there is no way of simply making it go away. The one thing about Simon which has struck Alan most strongly is that in addition to the inevitable slide into middle-age - being more heavy-set, possessor of a slight paunch, more florid about the face, jowly - he has lost his sense of humour. Not only is his old playfulness not evidenced in his manner and the way he seems to be going about things, it is totally absent from his eyes. Where there had once been a spark, Alan sees a void. The old Simon would have made a joke about 'Franco's', picking up on Alan's opening line; there would have been more humour, less spleen. Yet even so he hopes he is not a lost cause.

"You're probably right." Alan pauses, then changes tack. "When we used to come here, what was your favourite?"

"Favourite?"

"Flavour of ice cream. They had so many - and along with the various toppings they offered, you could choose some wicked combinations!"

"Did we come here often enough to have 'favourites'?" Although Simon sounds dubious, he gives it some thought. "Certainly none of those absurd things like 'Bubble Gum'!"

It is a statement which could have been delivered lightheartedly but comes across as condemnation.

"It was bright blue, wasn't it?" Alan tries again to set the tone.

"When I was growing up, 'Rum and Raisin' was the height of sophistication in our family - not that we had ice-cream very often. So, if we're talking 'favourites', I suppose I would have had that. Or possibly chocolate. But I can't really remember."

There had been numerous summer afternoons when the six of them had found their way to 'Gino's', Judith and Sebastian more often than not leading the charge. Alan recalls the pale green pistachio, the light brown honeycomb, and the long summer - was it their second or third? - when a challenge had been set to get through all the flavours on the menu in the shortest possible time. Gino, the proprietor, had provided 'loyalty cards' and they kept track of their progress meticulously. There is no surprise when Alan remembers it turning out to be a straight fight between Judith and Sebastian - and that, in spite of his apparent disinterest, he recalls Simon wholeheartedly participating for a while. Prompted by the memory, he turns slightly in his seat to look at the wall-mounted menu behind the counter half-expecting Espresso and Flat White to have suddenly reverted to Vanilla and Strawberry.

Examining his companion's profile, Simon struggles to see what all the fuss is about. To the best of his knowledge, enthusiasm had never been one of Alan's strong suits, which made Sharon's settling for him a surprise - almost more of a surprise than her rejection of him. If he were to turn to the family on the next table and ask them how old they thought Alan was, he wonders what they would say. He knows the two of them - along with Niamh and Judith - are contemporaries, and yet he sees in Alan a man who looks older than fifty-five and therefore someone over whom he is confident he has maintained an edge. Simon wonders what would have caused Alan to age more significantly than the rest of them? From his own perspective he had always assumed that his children wore him down, made him feel older than he actually was; but perhaps there is another side to that argument. Prompted by the sounds of families about them now, he is reminded of similar excursions, games in the park, the now-lost excitement of Christmas, and wonders if, somewhat paradoxically, children helped keep you young. If so, Alan had missed out on such rejuvenating opportunities, and although those times had existed for him in a relatively small window - between the beginning of the kids going to school and collapsing into teenage angst - in his more generous moments Simon is willing to give them some credit for having a positive impact on his own existence.

But it is more than that. Alan seems lifeless, as if he has locked himself into second-gear autopilot, resigned to living a life with everything even faintly remarkable removed. Neither of them can compare to Sebastian and Judith of course, but at least Simon feels he can give himself third prize for trying. Had Alan always been so uninspiring? During their time together they had been on a par, young men with similar interests and attitudes, twinned by ambition. Buoyed by the assessment of his present superiority, Simon is happy to concede he rarely felt particularly far ahead of Alan - though he was behind him on nothing. All of which again made Sharon's choice the more perplexing. What could Alan have possibly offered her that he could not? Perhaps it was precisely his mundane pliability which proved the trump card. Had she not always been the dominant one in the relationship, calling the shots, making the decisions? And did her throwing him over - on what was surely no more than a whim - demonstrate just how tenuous Alan's hold on her must have been? It feels like proof of a sort.

Simon glances to where Sebastian is engaged in debate with Niamh and Judith. Yes, Sebastian looks his age too, but at least the way he has lived has earned him that right; Simon has to give him some credit for that. Remembering the whirlwind he had been back then, he has never questioned how it was that Sebastian was able to succeed romantically where he had failed. If Alan ignites something akin to pity in Simon's eyes, his feelings toward Sebastian - far deeper and far less charitable - have, at their heart, nothing to do with romance nor Sharon and Judith. At all.

"I wanted to talk about London."

Alan's voice draws Simon back. He glances down at the table questioningly, as if it was his half-empty mug that had spoken.

"London?" he echoes. First ice cream and now a conversation about where they both live?

But Alan has a desire to be more specific.

"When we last met," he clarifies. "I know it was a long while ago now, but it was hardly satisfactory, was it?"

"A while ago?" Simon looks perplexed. "It's almost ancient history. Do you mean that time we were supposed to meet Niamh and she stood us up?" Alan nods. "Must be all of fifteen years ago."

"Nearer seventeen," Alan suggests, as if he has been keeping a log. "There was a disagreement of sorts."

"There was?"

Whether Simon is playing games with him or not, Alan finds his claim of innocence slightly difficult to swallow. Does he want him to confess to a sense of guilt or to offer up the sliver of a confession? If so, Alan is not inclined to do so.

"We argued about Sharon. About the past. About what happened here, with her, with us." Alan knows Simon cannot possibly have forgotten their original row when, once Sharon had declared for him, Simon had briefly lost control, overcome by incredulity. They had reprised the scene over dinner in Soho that evening, and even though the few intervening years between Sharon's choice and that London meeting had provided some anaesthetic, there had been no denying the heat her past actions continued to generate. Particularly for Simon.

"Right."

"It has always bothered me, Simon. It bothered me at the time, and it bothered me in London. It was so unlike us…" Alan wanted to say that it was so unlike Simon, but conciliation has a price. "And now she's gone, well, it seems fitting to bury the hatchet - don't you think?"

Simon's smile tries to convey the sense that he doesn't really know what Alan is talking about, attempting to demonstrate that Alan is the only one for whom this is an issue, that the suffering all one-sided.

"Nothing to forgive."

The word is deliberately chosen; Alan cannot fail to note it. If Simon imagines he is owed an apology, well, he has another think coming.

"Well then." Alan turns his attention to his own coffee, and even though he knows it not to be true, suggests: "Case closed."

§

Niamh & Simon

"I suppose we shouldn't be surprised," Niamh says breathlessly.

On leaving 'Franco's' Simon had set off with some purpose well ahead of the others, and she had needed to quicken her pace almost to a run to catch up to him. Her hand on his arm, along with her statement, slows him somewhat.

"Surprised by what, exactly?"

"Oh, you know," she buys a little time to re-establish a measure of equilibrium, "being back together again - all of us - thinking about the past."

"Not you too?"

"Why?" There is something hard in Simon's tone that surprises her.

"Alan was just going on about ice-cream; reminiscing about flavours or something."

His statement triggers a smile.

"Don't you remember though, the times we had in there? Oh not just there of course, but on the beach; lazy summer days, those dreadful games of frisbee when you and Seb would throw the thing so hard at us girls that we ended up in the sea!"

"Vaguely, I suppose - but apparently not as well as everyone else."

"'Gino's' was all part of those afternoons; the huge triple-scoop cones with the weirdest flavour combinations." She is disappointed Simon is not more enthusiastic. Perhaps he has chosen not to remember; perhaps it is all too frivolous for him now. She knows they have all moved on, but even so… "Weren't those great days, Simon?"

Her earnestness forces him to concede a little ground and he chooses to soften his tone; after all, he has no reason to be angry with her. There is nothing negative in their mutual history to eat away at him. Simon glances over his shoulder. Judith and Sebastian are walking together a little way behind, and further back Alan has stopped to look in a shop window.

"Yes, I suppose some of them were."

"And isn't that why we're here, to think about all of that?"

"The past, you mean?" He makes a show of debating the notion. "I thought we were here to think about Sharon. No-one seems to have talked about her that much; it seems to me it's all been about the rest of us."

"You may be right - but we shouldn't totally reject that should we, not when old friends get together for the first time in ages? Our collective past will inevitably hold sway over the present, at least for a little while. And anyway, Sharon will find a way of barging in at some point, won't she?"

Her proposition forces Simon to let a quiet laugh to escape, one that seems to have dug a tunnel under his defences and surfaced in open country. Niamh decides to push on.

"Do you remember that evening we all went to see 'Dirty Dancing' at the Odeon?" Simon groans, though this time not involuntarily. "You didn't like it?"

"Not that I recall." He knows he has seen it subsequently with Dawn - probably under duress. "Dreadful film."

"Why do you say that? I thought we all loved it."

"A little too saccharine for my taste, I'm afraid. And you know I was never a natural dancer."

Niamh laughs at the joke, Simon referencing the few times they went to a nightclub en masse along with his consequent demonstrations as to what being a totally uncoordinated man looked like. It feels a little like progress, a door slightly opened.

"And afterwards we went back to my place. Then Jude and Seb left, and after that Sharon and Alan drifted away."

Given his conversation in 'Franco's', hearing Sharon and Alan's names in the same sentence is almost enough to darken his mood once again, but there is something in Niamh's tone which suggests she is trying, and that she has something important she wants to say. He forces himself to relent; after all, he has news of his own and Niamh has quickly established herself as the only person with whom he is prepared to share it.

"We drank a little too much wine," he suggests, knowing he is on safe ground.

"Didn't we always?"

"That rough Italian stuff you and Sharon used to get by the gallon from the supermarket."

"How unfair!" Niamh laughs, infectiously.

They walk on for a few seconds, turning left and uphill a little. Alberta Avenue is not far away now.

"That night. You could have stayed." Unsure why she does so now, Niamh makes the admission she had never thought would pass her lips.

In the brief pause that follows Simon keeps his eyes fixed resolutely ahead. Unable to read him, his response surprises her.

"Don't think I don't know that."

"So why didn't you?" Her words escape not as a plea - it is surely too late for that - but as an epitaph to the person she had been. Perhaps the people they both had been. She wonders if, when remembering the past, her default approach is to translate events into feelings and it is these she wishes to rekindle, to experience again. In 'Franco's' she had listened to Judith and Seb bounce happenings and facts, people and places, back and forth as if they were engaged in some ultimately sterile tennis match. She knows such oneupmanship is not in her nature. And that evening, had she *really* wanted him to stay? She examines the phrase she used - "you could have stayed" - and knows she might have said something else; she might have said "I wanted you to stay". But had she? Can she remember her feelings from that night accurately enough to be sure

- not simply sure enough to replay what had been spoken, but to *know* what had been meant? Up to that point there had been no indication she and Simon would connect in that way. Perhaps she had felt sorry for him. Or sorry for herself. The two of them left on the shelf. Of course, a year later and Seb would turn the world upside down.

"Because I didn't know it at the time."

If he has been taken aback, Simon strives not to show it. He delivers his line without emotion, as if he were a professional actor asked to read from a bus timetable. But in spite of the words he has used - indeed, the words both of them have used - what does he really think? It is entirely feasible he would have been aware that Niamh might have been harbouring feelings for him; but what about from his side? Sharon and Alan had been together for about year by then, so his proposal to her - and to Judith come to that - was well beyond its sell-by date and had become invalid, immaterial. He liked Niamh, he always had, but the question was how much? Once the others had left that evening, had he been aware of the situation's potential or was his only preoccupation to leave too - because that is exactly what he did. Is what he has just told her true or is it a confection employed to kid them both? And why has she spoken now? Has she made her confession to 'clear the decks' or 'set the record straight'? Is it some knock-on from Sharon's demise, or has his presence, their coming together - all of them - resurrected more than the skeleton of memories? It would be easy enough to persuade himself such reincarnation is in play. He steals a glance at Niamh as she walks beside him, assuming she is trying to decide how to respond. Is there a chance that she has been burning a candle for him all this time? Is she about to restate those same words, changing their tense to "you could stay" because that is how she has always felt, and still does?

It is suddenly like a locus around which everything is spinning, not only his past, but potentially his future too - Dawn and the children notwithstanding. Or is that just him being fanciful, knocked off-balance by how things are now, by disappointment and frustration accumulated across the years, and bolstered by his immediate concerns, a cocktail causing him to misread the situation and fail to attribute the correct meaning to what she has said?

Niamh says nothing.

"I'm sorry."

Simon's apology, coming seemingly out of nowhere, takes Niamh by surprise; it hangs suspended in front of her seeking context.

"For what?" She thinks back to their 'Dirty Dancing' evening. Is he sorry he didn't stay? Is she glad he didn't?

"For my mood. Things have been…a little difficult recently. I may not be myself."

His statement is difficult for Niamh to parse given her only solid point of reference is thirty years in the past. There is no doubt that Simon is not the person he was then - none of them are - yet is that what he is apologising for, or is he saying that in some way he isn't even the person he appears to have become? If the former, then that is self-evident; if the latter, how is she supposed to measure it?

"I haven't been well for the last few months." He carries on. "Dawn had been pestering me to go and see our GP - if I'm honest, a florid and obnoxious man I can't stand - but eventually I gave in and went to see him about four weeks ago. It was the usual thing: blood pressure, blood tests, ECG. One of the tests came back slightly abnormal. At over four, the PSA was a little too high."

"Isn't that the test for…"

"Cancer, yes."

Simon beats her to the punch, almost as if he is embracing the word, as if he wants to own it, for it to be his. She is shocked, both at his statement and how pragmatically and unemotionally he has chosen to deliver it.

"So they sent me to the hospital for some more tests: a repeat PSA, some more bloods, a different scan. Double-checking, I suppose."

"And?"

"I don't know yet. I had hoped to hear before I came down - though if I had and, well…you know…I would probably have had to stay at home. Not for me so much as for Dawn. But I haven't heard and so I thought it might be good to get away, take my mind off things."

"And is it helping?" There is as much hope as question in Niamh's voice.

As they pause to cross the road, Simon already knows the answer. How can it be helping when all they want to do is to talk about the past and a time when he had been a different Simon, not just a better one but a healthier one? Being reminded of that - and all its associated present-tense negatives - is the last thing he needs right now: resurrection of his failure with Sharon and Judith, his animosity towards Alan, his distaste for Sebastian. And now the missed opportunity with Niamh - if that's what it was. These are mouldy cherries atop a rotting cake. Cancer or not, he has been eating himself from the inside for years now, never mind the rest of them. It has made him what he is - and what he has chosen to foist on Niamh and the others. He *is* himself, but at least he has a legitimate excuse to explain himself away.

He feels Niamh's hand on his arm again and remembers her question.

"Yes, a little."

And he wonders if he had been the one who had died, how many of them would have made a pilgrimage like this. It is another question to which he knows the answer.

§

Judith & Sebastian

"They've raced off," Judith says, pointing to Simon and Niamh marching on ahead.

"She probably wants to get the kettle on," Sebastian suggests mischievously, painting Niamh with a brush laden with domesticity.

Judith lets it go. It is an unfair assertion, bordering on rude; but Sebastian was always good at making such jokes, seeming to instinctively know where the boundary of unacceptability lay and then being prepared to step right up to it. Having spent the majority of the time in 'Franco's' interrogating him, she has already established that little appears to have changed; albeit circumstantial, his gentle barb in Niamh's direction is further evidence to support her theory. Based on how she had found Niamh - at heart the same, but clearly older, dumpier, more matronly - Judith had expected to find them all on a similar slide, hoping to stand out as the only one who has given time a run for its money. And on the face of it she has. Sebastian looks his age, just about; he has lines and wrinkles, freckles on his hands that didn't used to be there, grey beginning to establish itself in the hair above his ears and around his temples. Yet his is a weathering which suggests more than the simple passing of years - and thus simultaneously succeeds in affirming those things about him which have not altered. Yes, his hair may be greyer in places, but there is still a great deal of it, and he wears it in the same swept-back, rakish way he always had; his eyes may be framed by the odd deep line, but they retain something of the sparkle she had found so captivating; and while he is clearly not the physical specimen he once was, he still walks and carries himself with a certain swagger, an undiminished air of confidence in spite of everything. He has the aura of an ageing cavalier, as if he is still engaged in a war whose outcome is by no means decided; Athos still seeking to outwit the wicked Cardinal - or perhaps a Hugh Grant figure still aspiring to make movies like "Notting Hill" thirty years on. Judith has always had a soft spot for Hugh Grant.

If she wants to damn Sebastian for remaining attractive she finds she cannot quite bring herself to do so.

"Have you spoken to Simon much?" she asks instead.

"Not really. A little bit on the way to the cemetery; the odd word on the way down from there to here. Why?"

"How have you found him?" She ignores his question and pushes on with her own line of enquiry.

"Honestly?"

"Of course. Why not honestly?"

Sebastian glances over his shoulder to confirm Alan is out of earshot.

"Grumpy. I think that's how I'd describe him. He acts like a man who's swallowed something unpleasant and is prepared to blame everyone else for it."

Judith laughs.

"Is that unfair?" Sebastian asks, though with an air suggesting he doesn't really care what she thinks.

"No, just funny." She pauses. "That's not how you remember him?"

"Simon?" He gives her question due consideration. "I don't think so. I mean, he was never at the top of my Christmas card list or anything like that -"

"And vice versa," Judith interjects.

"Indeed. But I'd like to think there were occasional high points, especially in the beginning." Sebastian looks ahead, as if seeking validation of his statement from clues offered by Simon's back as he walks some way ahead of them. "But not many," he qualifies, as if finding one or two.

There is a moment's silence as they continue on, Judith resisting the urge to pause and look in the window of Seasalt as they pass by. She has more important things on her mind.

"And how do you remember me?"

Sebastian looks at her and laughs.

"What's so funny?" she asks, her tone betraying surprise at his response.

"Nothing at all," he smiles, "it's such a big question, isn't it? Considering… I mean, I remember you in all sorts of ways and at different times, in differing circumstances. It doesn't have a single answer, does it? How would you answer the question if I asked it of you?"

Knowing he is being rhetorical, Judith chooses not to respond. She does so in part to avoid gifting him an opportunity to protect himself by not giving her a proper answer, but her main motivation is to prevent herself from revealing too much. It could be damaging were she to give him any indication that she regards the present-day Sebastian to be surprisingly close to the one she had known back then. Close, at least from her perspective.

Sebastian realises Judith is not going to take the bait.

"I remember you much as you are now - physically, that is. Slim, elegant, attractive, sexy. If you're fishing for compliments Jude, that's the best you're going to get!"

They both laugh.

"You're too gallant," she says, the last word heavily accented in the the French manner.

"But most of all I remember the fun, the fights, the highs and lows… I assume it must be the same for you, given our relationship was such a rollercoaster for a while. We seemed to swing wildly between the extremes of some kind of spectrum didn't we? Liking and loathing."

"Loving and hating?" she suggests.

Having briefly lost sight of Niamh and Simon, they turn a corner to find them crossing the road ahead.

"There is something of a gap though," Sebastian continues, ignoring Judith's undisguised trap.

"Oh, what's that?"

"When you left. *Why* you left. I know we were," he pauses momentarily to try and find a good enough phrase, "not in the best of places at the time, but it seemed to me as if you were there and then suddenly you weren't. I know *where* you went - to London of course - and the reason for your going - the chance of a new career - but I don't think I ever quite *understood* it. Does that make sense?"

Weighing the merits and demerits of attempting to decipher Sebastian's phrase 'not in the best place at the time', Judith decides to leave it unmolested. It warrants clarification and to be garnished with her own overlay on how their relationship had been at that point - or how it had already ceased to be 'a thing' altogether. She suddenly wonders if she ever really told him exactly what she thought about how he behaved in those last couple of months before she fled to her new life - and instantly knows she did not. But now is the not the time for that. Nor is it the time to be totally honest about her departure, nor - no matter what she might have said contemporaneously - how uncertain her future was likely to be. She had been prepared to take risks - and indeed took some of them! - in order to escape from him. Having already toyed with the idea of leaving - even to the somewhat desperate extent of exploring options for a transfer within the bank - when an alternative door opened just a fraction, she felt compelled to barge her way through it.

"I daresay you understood it more than you make out, Seb," she says, somewhat cryptically. "As far as I was concerned the bank was beginning to feel like a dead-end. Oh, the work was okay I suppose, and the people nice enough, but there didn't seem that much of a future in it." Nor, she might have added, a future with him. And if there still had been, what might she have done then? "Because I'd been working on the corporate side of things during the first part of '88 I'd met all sorts of interesting people and had dealings with various companies. Most of them were mundane commercial outfits of course... Anyway, one day I had a call from a guy called Max who ran a production company which specialised in making ads; not just for TV, but ads for magazines, posters, that sort of thing. He asked me if I'd ever thought of a career in front of the camera."

"'In front of the camera'? Sounded a bit dodgy, don't you think?"

"Yes," she laughs, "that's exactly what I *did* think. Anyway, the next time I had a meeting with them - the company I mean - Max brought along one of their creative directors, Frank. They took me to lunch; buttered me up I suppose. Asked if I'd like to do a photoshoot, no commitment on either side. So a couple of weeks later, I did. That must have been, I don't know, July or August. They were really pleased with the outcome, sent me a copy of some of the shots; I liked them too. When they offered me a contract in September, well, I was already sold on the idea."

"September." Sebastian tries to relocate himself back in time.

"It was that simple," Judith says, omitting any reference to the circumstances which might have helped propel her forward - and the fact that the offer they'd made her had, at best, been vague and open to interpretation. Or abuse. "It seemed an opportunity too good to miss. Already having something in mind they said they'd like to use me on, they needed a quick decision, and that was what I gave them. After that it was a bit of a whirlwind. I handed my notice in at the bank and four weeks later, well…"

"We had that hastily arranged leaving party. Rightly or wrongly I remember it for being a somewhat tense affair - and for me getting horribly drunk."

"Not that the latter was unheard of," she suggests.

"Touché."

It had not been the exit Judith had expected; perhaps until that point she had never considered leaving. Not that she would confess it now, but she knew there had been a part of her - the now defunct incurably romantic part of her - that clung to the assumption the two of them would eventually calm down and find a level; that they would settle into each other once and for all and stop the violent swings between all and nothing and back again. For a while Sebastian had felt like the kind of man who would suit her well enough - though later she wondered just how much her seduction had been second-hand, baited by the fame attached to his father and the consequent prospect of minor pubic recognition. At least she is honest enough to understand how such associations have come to appeal to her; after all, she has accumulated more than enough evidence to conclusively prove the case.

"Two months later you were off too. I'm sorry I missed your do, but by then things were already hectic for me in London."

"You didn't miss much."

Judith, expecting a little more, presses on.

"And then, before you can say 'Robinson Crusoe', it's three years later and you're married and all the rest of it."

He laughs half-heartedly.

"No-one was more surprised than me. And there wasn't really any 'the rest of it', not in the sense of 'Happy Ever After' anyway. Or happy anything. Almost the opposite, in fact."

"The way you talk about it... Sounds - I don't know - like you made a massive mistake."

They turn into Alberta Avenue. Ahead, Sebastian sees Niamh and Simon divert from the pavement in favour of the path to her front door. They will be all back together again soon enough, a brief confirmation of plans before they separate and then later reconvene for the meal that evening.

"Eight years of mistake as it turned out." He dives into précis in order not to leave any loose ends dangling. "Melissa is a wonderful woman - for someone else that is. No matter how hard I tried we could never connect the way we needed to; certainly not well enough to make it work." He judges the shortening distance to Niamh's front gate. "It would have been better for both of us had I found a way to bail out earlier, instead of being thrown out later."

Sebastian is assaulted by the ghosts haunting what he has just said; how much of that brief summary could he apply to his relationship with Judith? And if, in the intervening years, he has been able to apply such a parallel, then surely Judith must have done so too - even with limited facts about him and Melissa at her disposal. He holds the gate open to let her through and then excuses himself from immediately following, begging a few minutes for a cigarette: "an old and disgusting habit I picked up at some point and into which I collapse from time to time". Watching her as she disappears into the house, he finds himself drawn again into the comparison which, although it is one he is always reluctant to make, he finds inevitable. Indeed he probably began to resurrect it once again the previous evening in 'The Busted Flush'.

The daughter of an old friend of his father's, he and Melissa had been thrown together across a number of parties as the eighties turned into the nineties. Sebastian is unable to deny there had been a degree of mutual but slightly unbalanced attraction, an itch they had mutually chosen to scratch on more than one occasion before things got serious. Events were to demonstrate that his father, in endeavouring to help by encouraging them on and extolling the virtues of wedded bliss to his son, merely lit a slow fuse that would run its course a few years later. Only too well aware that his professional life had lurched from one disappointment to another, perhaps he had grasped too quickly at the particular straw Melissa represented, an impulsive move given credence by his father's endorsement. Once they were married his life settled into a normality of sorts, and to this day Sebastian is unable to identify precisely when things began to unravel. But unravel they did. They had moved home twice during their crumbling marriage in the hope that a change of scenery might come to their rescue; they had talked of children, but for one reason or another none materialised. Towards the end, Melissa vacillated between regret - claiming offspring would have been the glue to hold them together - and professing gratitude that they hadn't created a child who would have to suffer as a result of Sebastian's implosion. For that was how she saw it. And though factually her ground was solid enough - he had strayed more than once during the summer of ninety-eight before becoming a serial philanderer early the following year - Sebastian still views Melissa herself as the catalyst for his betrayal, even if he can't locate the precise event which sparked it.

As he drags the warm smoke from his cigarette into his lungs, he knows pursuit of any notion of catalyst is where a parallel with Judith falls down: she did nothing to trigger his behaviour that final summer. Perhaps he'd had enough of the on-off experience with her; perhaps the lurching from one position to another, one state to another, gradually wore him down; perhaps it all became too much like hard work. He tells himself that it wasn't going back into battle with her which was the problem, but rather the prospect of doing so to gain so little ground. At times his relationship with Judith felt more like trench warfare than anything else, each of them claiming small amounts of turf before being forced to give it back. And the periods of peace in between were not exactly that; they were simply quieter times which allowed him to get his breath back before needing to go over the top once again. Then one day the notion that there must have been easier skirmishes to fight assailed him, and as soon as it had, first Sharon and then Niamh ended up in his sights. Neither he nor they had stood a chance.

Even now he doesn't understand how - in either general or specific terms - he hoped to benefit from two ultimately meaningless local conquests. In proving a point - to both himself and Judith - had he expected those minor engagements to somehow gain him ground when it came to reengaging with Judith? Or perhaps he thought they might serve to reestablish both his supremacy and invincibility, and in doing so prove sufficient to make her come to her senses. Either way, it was soon plain enough that there were to be no positive outcomes: after that final fiery blaze, Judith simply quit the field - and then the town altogether. When Sebastian discovered that she and he had collectively destroyed the fabric of his life there - including his relationships with the rest of them - he knew he had to leave too. If there was any consolation to be had it came in the form of him telling himself it had been time to move on anyway, all Judith had done was to precipitate his departure.

For most men his coming off the rails with Judith would have proved a lesson learned, one which could have been applied in some way, shape or form when it came to Melissa. For most men, but not him. Generalising and manufacturing similarly unsatisfactory scenarios for others and placing them in it, Sebastian has no hesitation in awarding both Simon and Alan the lowest-grade 'most men' award - but then he reminds himself that neither of them would have had the wherewithal to get themselves into such a tantalising situation in the first place. Such knowledge is strangely comforting, and in spite of the outcomes - with both Judith and Melissa - he can only regard his failures (if, indeed, that's what they were) as proof of his superiority.

The Evening

Niamh, Judith, Alan, Simon & Sebastian

"Sharon left some instructions," Niamh says as soon as there is a lull in the conversation, the orders having been placed and the exact location and state of the toilets verified.

They had arrived at the restaurant more or less simultaneously, disembarking from two taxis, Alan and Simon having taken one from the ferry, the rest coming from Niamh's house where Sebastian's car was now parked just across the road from Judith's. 'The Supper Place' - its calligraphy encouraging the misreading of 'super' in preference to 'supper' - was a little way out of town, a previously ramshackle suite of ex-farm buildings that he been sympathetically converted into a bistro. Once the farmhouse itself, the main building housed a 'premium' dining room and the kitchens; the remainder of the footprint - the old stables and byres - had been designed to facilitate more relaxed eating, and boasted a myriad of little nooks and crannies all connected by a modern glass corridor which skirted the main yard and provided access to and from the kitchens. Having scouted it well in advance, Niamh had managed to secure a discrete corner of an ex-feed store. It was like having their own private function room.

Not without a little frisson of excitement, the initial chatter had inevitably been about the restaurant itself, the menu, and whether any of them could remember what the place had been when they were last quorate. "A working farm," Niamh had said at one point when Sebastian was away in the gents. "It went into decline in the nineties and was abandoned for a while before the current owners bought it about six years ago." They agreed it had been a masterstroke, "especially if the food is good" Alan suggested. And so they had embarked on the standard ritual of ordering drinks, perusing the menu, making their choices. It was only once their server had left that silence fell.

"Instructions?" echoed Alan.

"How typically Sharon," laughed Sebastian, already more than half-way through his first glass of wine.

Niamh knew all eyes were on her.

"Perhaps instructions isn't the most appropriate word." She paused slightly guilty at her white lie, knowing that instructions was exactly what they were. The first thing Sharon had insisted upon was that - 'The Supper Room' being her suggestion - not only did they find a table that was reasonably private but it also needed to be round. "I don't want anyone - mentioning no names - taking it upon themselves to sit at the head of the table and dominate proceedings. Nor anyone to hide away at the back come to that." Niamh had suggested it all sounded very democratic, to which Sharon had replied "not while I'm in charge!" And now there they were, sitting in a circle, equidistant from each other; Alan on her left, then Sebastian and Simon with Judith to her right. Niamh carried on. "I think she just wanted to have some influence, as if she was here herself. Does that make any sense?"

"Are we behaving ourselves so far?" Sebastian asked. "I don't want to be sent to the naughty step."

They laughed dutifully.

"Anyway, she wanted me to start with something about herself before - she said - we all took over."

"You make it sound like a revolution," Simon said.

"The Peasants' revolt." Sebastian again.

"You know how these things go, how an evening can run away with you." Niamh tried to spread her gaze evenly around the table but it lingered a little longer on Sebastian than anyone else. "And we're supposed to be here for Sharon, not us, so I think it's only right that she gets first shout."

"And how are we going to do that?" Alan asked.

"She wanted me to start by telling you something about her, something about her childhood; things you're unlikely to be aware of."

"And were you?" Judith asked. "Aware of them I mean, before she told you what she wanted you to say."

"A little." Niamh takes a sip of her wine, slightly concerned she is inserting herself into the evening at the very beginning. But perhaps there is no way to avoid that. "After all, we shared a house for well over twenty years - except for her time with Malcolm - so it's inevitable I'm going to know her better than everyone else. But I wasn't aware of all of it."

"In the same way that we don't know the totality of each other's story." Trying to be supportive, Judith looks round the table.

"We'll know some of it," Alan suggests.

"Of course. But the gaps are going to be enormous - just as they are between us and Sharon."

"Cavernous," Simon concurs, "though there hasn't been much opportunity or desire to fill them in, has there? Which makes it all rather…"

"Some of us have had more 'coverage' than others," Sebastian interrupts him and raises his glass in Judith's direction, "though whether that's a help or hindrance I've no idea." Although he has claimed indifference, it is clear he as a view on the matter.

"Perhaps," Alan interjects before Judith can respond, "we should let Niamh get on; I for one would like to know what Sharon wanted to tell us."

They all look Niamh's way again.

"Oh don't get your hopes up!" She laughs to herself. "I think she just wanted to get things started."

"A kind of amuse-bouche," Judith suggests, trying to be helpful.

Sebastian drains his glass and reaches for the white wine. "Who's paying for all this, by the way?"

Heads turn Niamh's way again.

"I am." She hesitates. "Or rather, Sharon is. I'm just her…"

"Representative on Earth?" Simon offers, his tone vaguely sarcastic.

Accompanied only by the sound of wine refilling Sebastian's glass, a short silence descends as if Simon has succeeded in reminding them why they are all there. It is the cue Niamh needs.

"Did you know Sharon's middle name was Mary? It was one of those small facts she said contributed to make her who she was. Or that, when she was thirteen she decided to have her hair cut short as a protest against her parents - for what reason she didn't say - and liked it that way so much that she never grew it long again."

"She used to have long hair?" Judith is unable to contain her surprise.

"Yes, who'd have thought? She showed me a photograph," Niamh smiled, "one of her old school photos; the kind, long forgotten about, you keep at the bottom of a box or the back of a drawer. She looked very pretty - you know, in a girly way."

"And you'd never really think of her as 'girly'." Judith again.

"Not that she wasn't pretty," said Alan, the tone in his voice challenging them to deny it.

"And none of which stopped her from liking the odd practical joke," Niamh said, triggering private memories for all of them. "She wanted to apologise if she ever went too far; she never meant any harm, and I don't think she caused any, not really. But then I seem to have largely been exempt, a mere observer looking on."

For a moment Niamh expects one of them to step in with their own story. Sharon's practical jokes were never rudimentary or crude - like swapping salt for sugar - but were always targeted, attempting to correct behaviour or make others see when they were being ridiculous. Niamh knows if she were allow the others into the flow now her momentum would be lost so she hurries on.

"And she confessed to having few regrets. Malcolm was the biggest one. I asked her if he hadn't been a mistake, but she admitted to no mistakes." Niamh makes the effort to smile at the three men in turn. "Some of us might want to challenge that, but that wasn't how she saw things. She said decisions - all decisions - were simply what moved you forward, took you from one place to the next, and that if you didn't make any decisions no-one would get anywhere. I think that was how her logic worked."

"I've heard that somewhere else," Alan said, "though I can't remember where." Simon nods as if he knows the source but chooses to say nothing.

"And children."

"What about children, Niamh?" Judith interrupts.

"One of her regrets. Though she admitted to being conflicted there. Personally I don't think she was totally convinced she regretted not having any. Unsurprisingly she was certainly glad none came along with Malcom, though at thirty-eight she felt she was too old by then anyway. But earlier? There was no reason she hadn't had any, not that I know."

"Other than the failure to find someone suitable to father them?" Given the company, it is a suggestion perhaps only Judith can legitimately make, and even though she appears to do so without the desire to apply a veneer of any kind, each of the men cannot avoid silently taking up a brush to add their own individual coating. Alan particularly.

"I don't know. Who can say?" Niamh shakes her head just a little; glances down to her wine. "Perhaps it had something to do with her own childhood, her parents. You know, the thing with her hair."

"Her childhood hadn't been happy?" Alan asks.

"Not especially. At least, that's what she told me." Niamh pauses. "Did you know she had a brother?"

"A brother?" Alan again, though any one of them could have echoed Niamh's words and the tone of surprise would have largely been the same.

"James. He was older. When she was eleven he drowned after swimming too far out to sea. I didn't know about him until just before she died. She told me she'd idolised him, and that the accident tore her family apart. I suppose it must have changed her perspective on life." Niamh goes on. "Her parents were never the same after that. Sharon said being the only one left changed how they behaved with her, with each other. Instead of the tragedy making her more precious, it was as if they were blaming her for what happened."

"Maybe that had something to do with that thing with her hair," Judith observes, briefly interrupting Niamh.

"Perhaps. She said that for all of them life and love began to leak away. It was why she never went to university."

"I did wonder," Sebastian said. "I knew she'd never been, and she was clearly bright enough."

"As soon as she was old enough to leave school, leave home, get a job, she did - which meant no A-levels, because A-levels would have involved another two years at home. I asked her why she didn't go away altogether, move somewhere else in the country; but she didn't answer. Maybe, in spite of it all, she felt tied here. Anyway, the hospital offered a desperate sixteen-year-old a way out." Niamh smiled. "I think she was a little rebellious for a while, before we met her."

Judith smiles. "Rebellious, really? You wouldn't have known it. She always seemed so sorted and sensible."

"Perhaps she'd worked that rebelliousness out of her system before we met her," Alan suggests to the table in general.

"Maybe so," says Niamh.

"Those practical jokes of hers were probably left over from the Sharon she'd once been," Simon offers. "I'm sure we've all one or two painful examples we could quote. There were times she could be quite - sharp."

Sebastian's sudden laugh surprises them all. "But wasn't she just brilliant though?!"

As if it had been coordinated, five hands reach for five glasses and raise them to five sets of lips.

"So is that where we're supposed to start?"

Simon's question coincides with the arrival of their starters, the table a sudden flurry of activity with two black-and-white clad servers placing soup, terrine, and salmon appropriately in front of them. Had they been confused by Simon's query, they show no immediate signs of having done so.

"That's a first," Simon says once the staff have moved away.

"What is?" Judith asks.

"Getting each of our orders right - and without the need to ask or check."

"Perhaps it's a good sign," she suggests. "I mean, a sign that they know what they're doing and that the food will be good. Bon appétit."

A modest symphony comprising the gentle clinking of cutlery on crockery then ensues, punctuated by the odd unintelligible murmur or explicit statement confirming the quality of the food.

"What did you mean, Simon?" Niamh asks between spoonfuls of spiced parsnip soup.

"About it being a first? I though we'd covered that one."

"No; your question about it being where we were supposed to start. What did you mean by that?"

They look at him as he finishes a mouthful of terrine, and, conscious of the attention, he takes the opportunity to extend the moment by lifting his glass from the table.

"All that stuff about Sharon's background, her childhood. Was that a starter of sorts too? If you've finished telling us what she wanted us to know, does she expect us to use that as a prompt? What 'instruction' did she give you?"

Niamh ignores the implied parenthesis.

"None really." She thinks for a moment then smiles. "But it is funny to think of what she said - or what she wanted me to say - as a kind of 'starter'. Don't you think so? Considering."

"I can't wait for the main course!" Sebastian laughs.

"But you wouldn't put it past her - implicitly making that kind of a connection, knowing what we'd be likely to do with it," says Judith. "It would be something else to demonstrate just how canny she was."

There is another murmur, a blurring of specific comment and words indistinctly uttered, all of which are sufficient to indicate that Judith may indeed have a point. As the sounds of lifting food from plates and bowls gradually dwindles, Alan is the one who steps into the breach.

"I'll happily go first," he says.

"Go first?" Simon asks.

"If that's what she wanted us to do - to follow her lead, I mean - then I'll pick up the baton. Unless Niamh wants to, of course." He looks at her. "After all, I think I'm probably the next logical choice, don't you?"

Even though it is a rhetorical question and delivered more as statement of fact than a challenge, Alan can't help but glance round the table to see if there is anyone who disagrees with him. He would give way to Niamh, but his relationship with Sharon surely allows him to claim the high ground, even if the others feel they have their own individual justifications for being advanced in the packing order. If anyone is uncertain on exactly what his 'logic' is based, they say nothing. Alan's glance comes to rest on Sebastian.

"Fill your boots," Sebastian says, smiling, "we have to start somewhere. Are you going to tell us something else we don't know?"

"Not intentionally. I simply thought I'd take my lead from Sharon and tell you a little about my own childhood."

"Really?" Simon sounds surprised.

"It's a safe place to start I think," Alan says, "rather than trying to plunge in to something more deep and meaningful."

"Especially as we're all still very sober!" Sebastian's joke is suitably appreciated, a fact he celebrates by topping up his wine glass once again.

"How is it a 'safe place to start'?" Niamh speaks for them all.

"Because it was normal. No tragedies or dramas, no-one who was famous -" he nods towards Sebastian.

"Or infamous," Judith counters.

"Unfair, unfair!" pleads Sebastian in a tone of mock-hurt.

"No-one of any renown then," Alan modifies his statement. "In fact, I suppose my childhood was entirely 'average', 'middle of the road'. Not that its being unremarkable was a bad thing, you understand. I did well enough at school, okay at University. It wasn't the kind of upbringing to suggest you'd see me uproot any trees along the way." He pauses. "Not that you're surprised by any of that, of course. It's the mould you might have expected to have made me."

"How so?" Niamh asks.

Alan laughs; a short private laugh he does not expect to be picked up by the rest of them. It is not.

"Because of how I used to be, I suppose. Let's face it, I was never the one to suggest things, to try things out. A follower, not a leader. 'Adventure' was most certainly not my middle name."

They smile.

"Maybe that's what resonated with Sharon," Niamh suggests, taking on the role of pilot, steering the conversational vessel of her old friend's making. "Given what she'd been through when she was younger, perhaps she appreciated your solid reliability. Maybe she wasn't as 'sorted' as we liked to think she was. You might have helped her with that."

Whether Judith, Sebastian or Simon agree with her no not, they say nothing. With all eyes turned to Alan, he owes Niamh a response.

"If so, she never said - at least not in any way that I could interpret as such. But then I've never been that imaginative either. Perhaps that's why insurance - and underwriting in particular - suits me so well."

"How so?" Judith once again acts as Niamh's 'wing man'.

"Because it requires a certain skillset - and a lack of other personal traits - in order to be successful. For example, you need to have a particular view of risk in order to be good at it, and I think I have that; growing up, our family was very risk averse. It's not a job for everyone."

"You don't say."

Whether intended or not, it is impossible for them not to interpret Simon's comment as barbed, layered with much that is related to Alan and almost nothing to do with the underwriting profession itself.

"For example," Alan chooses to sidestep the implication, "can you see Seb as an underwriter, sitting behind a desk, weighing and judging risk? Isn't he more likely to be the sort of character insurers would want to steer clear of?"

Delivered lightly, it is a notion that raises a laugh - especially from Sebastian himself. When the moment passes, Alan takes the opportunity to counter.

"Actually, you might make a good underwriter, Simon."

"Me! I hated the bloody insurance company, couldn't wait to get out."

"Maybe so," Alan says, "but I'm not talking about the company specifically. Don't you have a logical mind, the ability to compare one thing with another without emotion getting in the way? Can't you distance yourself from a subject when you need to? Those are all necessary for a good underwriter."

Simon glances round the table to see how the others have responded to Alan's suggestion. Unaware of the mine Alan has placed in his path, he feels responsibility settling on him.

"But what was it you said? Something about needing not to have specific traits too? I'm sure if I wanted to I could come up with a few things that would disqualify me on a number of fronts."

"I expect most of us could," Judith offers.

Simon ignores her comment.

"And anyway, I didn't have the kind of solid foundation you enjoyed, Alan. My childhood - if that's where we're starting - was nowhere near as average as yours. If anything, it was closer to Sharon's."

"In what way?" Niamh asks.

"In not being particularly happy. There was no tragedy or anything like that - I was an only child, after all - but it was far from plain sailing."

"But you were academically okay," Judith observes, a mild sense of challenge in both her voice and choice of words, "and unlike Sharon you went to university, got a degree."

"Yes, that's true of course, but underneath that achievement lay the heart of the issue." Simon takes a sip of wine then continues, his tone more matter-of-fact. "I was the first in my family to get to university. Historically we were little more than common labourers. I grew up alongside cousins who couldn't spell or read properly, who struggled with maths. Probably struggled with living, when I come to think of it. They were brutish some of them - and not just the boys! Destined for a life behind bars. But I wasn't like that. I was just that little bit brighter - enough to make me stand out. And being different made me not a little afraid; you know, worried that one day someone would turn on me because I wasn't like them and they couldn't work me out. Or because they were jealous or something. Their response in such situations always tended to the physical, unpleasantly so."

"I didn't know," said Niamh.

"No-one knew," Simon's retort is blunt, "though I may have told Sharon, I can't remember. It's not the sort of thing you shout from the rooftops."

"But didn't your parents help protect you?" There is a marginally softer tone in Alan's voice. "Wouldn't they have been on your side?"

"You'd think. But they didn't understand either; they couldn't see what was going on. My mother would undermine my achievements at school because she didn't recognise how important they were. She'd never pester me to do homework but rather would try and lure me away from it, to do something with her that she thought was more fun. Fun for her I mean. I was even encouraged - and occasionally forced - to skive off from school... So in a way they were worse than the rest of the clan because when I needed to be able to lean on them I couldn't."

"That part does sound a bit like Sharon's experience," Niamh says. "Strange the parallels that exist between people."

"Which is why I think I may have told her," Simon responds. "But then given what you said earlier about us not knowing, perhaps I just made that up - because of the connection. Was there a parallel between us? Of sorts I suppose, given I couldn't wait to get away from home too. My parents were idiots and I was surrounded by imbeciles."

"And you're not." Sebastian's phrase escapes from his mouth almost as if it was unready to do so; it sounds unfinished, unable to decide if it is a statement or a question, whether it relates to Simon's parents or the people he used to be surrounded by. Or is surrounded by now. Was it a comment about the five of them, here and now, or an observation about Simon himself? As the others try and decipher what Sebastian meant, he empties his glass once more, glancing to where a member of staff is now approaching their table ready to remove their empty plates and bowls.

"Was everything alright for you?" The waiter's inevitable question, chirpily delivered, acts as a firebreak. Had Simon been inclined to interpret Sebastian's comment in the most negative way possible, his next contribution would surely have been less moderated than the one he chooses to deliver about a minute later.

"You never had any trouble of that kind, did you Seb?"

"Of what kind?" Sebastian looks up from his wine-pouring duties which, on this occasion, also includes the glasses of both Niamh and Judith.

"A difficult childhood. You were never surrounded by dolts and dullards; undoubtedly quite the opposite. Thanks to your father, you probably had just about anything you could ever want."

"I'm not sure I'd go that far," Sebastian replies.

"Oh come on, Seb!" Heads turn toward Judith. "Your childhood was nothing like Sharon's or Simon's or mine. Or Niamh's, probably. Because of your dad - the famous Hugh Stephenson - everything was cushioned for you; you told me that yourself. The public schools, the holidays, the limelight. You were never short of cash - or love, I suspect - and had the sort of freedom which allowed you to do pretty much exactly what you wanted; something most people can only dream about."

Sebastian's face darkens just a shade.

"Well, if I said all that, Jude, then it must be true." He tries a smile which surfaces as mildly unconvincing. "But it wasn't as much plain sailing as you might think; for example, I'm not sure freedom and public schools necessarily go hand-in-hand." He pauses to gather his thoughts. "Did I suffer the kind of tragedy Sharon faced with her brother? No. And was my upbringing in any way like Simon's from the point of view of support or intelligence or any of those other things? Again no. And certainly not like yours." Heads turn in Judith's direction, but Sebastian doesn't give her time to bite. "If you want to equate my upbringing with some kind of serene progress through life then I can't stop you - any of you - from thinking that; but Jude, you know more about how it really was than you let on."

There is a short pause, four pairs of eyes looking at Judith to see if she is going to pick up the gauntlet Sebastian seems to have thrown down. In response she merely lifts her glass from the table and takes a sip of wine.

"Can you enlighten us, Seb?" Inevitably it is Niamh who asks the question, refusing to let any tension build. "To be fair to Jude, I think we've all made assumptions about your early life, how privileged it must have been - on some level, at least. And I don't think you've ever done anything to disabuse us of that fact."

"If it is indeed a fact," Alan offers an escape route should he need one, yet Sebastian doesn't miss a beat.

"Yes, I suppose it is a fact. And I suppose I never did anything to disabuse you of your perceptions of how you assumed it was. I mean, why should I? Wouldn't you have done the same thing? There are benefits to being thought of in a certain way..." Sebastian leaves the statement hanging. If it is cryptic, there is a sense that it may have defeated all of them, himself included. "But don't think all that fluff - the schools, the holidays, the famous father etcetera - didn't mean there weren't pressures too."

"Such as?" The tone in Simon's voice suggests there is some way to go before he will be convinced Sebastian ever suffered any degree of childhood discomfort.

"It all revolves around my dad, of course." Sebastian pauses, conscious he has shifted down a gear. It is an unnatural sensation pacing himself in such a way, but he feels a sense of obligation - though whether to his friends or to himself he is unsure. Perhaps it is duty to his father. "He had this image didn't he? Or multiple images, I suppose. Still does. The flying winger, the international sportsman. He was a natural - both rugby player and winner - and that combination, allied to the fact that he possessed a certain charisma, made it inevitable that people, the media, would latch onto him." He pauses to allow himself a smile. "As a kid it was wonderful. My dad was this superstar... And so I became the son of a superstar, some of that pixie dust rubbed off on me."

"And you loved it." This time there is no malice in Judith's comment, partly because she is closest to understanding how intoxicating such a situation can be. He smiles at her across the table.

"How could I not? It was like suddenly finding out you were royalty; you know, as if you were one of those people who'd done their ancestry thing and discovered they were descended from Henry the Eighth or someone. Don't ask if that spoiled me because I don't even know what that means… And then dad migrated from professional player to professional pundit, and then to this new kind of celebrity he created for himself. Or had created for him. Sports shows, game shows, reality shows, interviews, tv ads, even travelogues. And the money flooded in, and mum and I - right up until she died - just rolled with the punches, took advantage of the spin-offs, the benefits."

"That still doesn't sound too much like pressure to me," Simon says, only mildly mollified by Sebastian's tone.

"You're right, Simon; no pressure there at all. At least on the face of it. People used to ask me - in fact, Jude, I remember you asking me the first time you met him - whether there was any difference between the public and the private Hugh Stephenson. And there wasn't. Not a jot. Although I didn't see it then, this meant I wasn't living with a traditional father but with a different kind of person entirely. His aura, his presence, was unrelenting. I had nowhere to turn to get away from 'the Stephenson Rocket'. At some point I think love was replaced by hero worship - and that's where the pressure came. I felt I had to live up to him. It was as if he set a standard, and though he never said as much, it was a standard he expected me to meet. Or maybe it was more the case that I thought it was one he expected me to meet. So talk about the holidays and the schools if you like, but behind it all was this deepening fear of failure, of not living up to … him, I suppose." The others wait while Sebastian takes a drink of water. "Wrong glass!" he jokes. "Anyway, I found I started giving myself goals to satisfy this need to prove myself worthy. Inevitably they were sporty goals at first, but I found I was too slow to be a sprinter, too inept to be a footballer. People thought I'd be a natural rugby player, but I wasn't strong enough - or brutal enough. Dad didn't seem to mind, said it didn't matter. So then I thought of other things, academic mainly. But in the end I was no more than passable there too. I was breezing through life, living this privileged existence on the back of my father, and all the while there was a nagging and multiplying doubt that I was fundamentally average. And not good enough for him." From the corner of his eye Sebastian sees the waiters approaching with their main courses. "I suppose I'm still trying to find my niche, to satisfy the need to live up to my dad, whether he wants or expects me to or not."

If Sebastian finds the waiters' intrusion a relief he does not say so, but instead goes into his routine of being chatty with the staff, making them laugh. Glancing up from their newly arrived main courses and catching a glimpse of him in full flow, how many of them would equate the showman they see before them as being a slice of his father, 'a chip off the old block'? Is there a part of Sebastian which is *exactly* like Hugh, and has he been able to emulate at least one element of his father's character without realising it? A test passed. Niamh can certainly see it. In microcosm, it offers her a reprise of that affable charm to which both she and Sharon succumbed, if only for the shortest possible time. She can also see how easy it would have been for Judith to have been caught in that web too. Once the initial round of comments about steak, fish and risotto have subsided, it is her desire to make this latter connection concrete which prompts her to speak.

"What did you mean, Jude, when you said Seb's upbringing had been nothing like yours?"

Judith looks up from where she is removing a small bone from a sliver of trout.

"Did I say that? I thought all I said was that Seb thought his had been unlike everyone's."

"But he seemed so definite in your case. You *were* definite, Seb, weren't you?"

Having had Niamh's attention turned back to him, Sebastian allows a fork-full of steak to hover above his plate.

"Was I?" He glances at Judith and then back to Niamh. "It's not really my place to comment at all. It's up to Jude whether she wants to get onto this little merry-go-round of childhood reminiscence." Sebastian smiles in Judith's direction. He has offloaded what, in his father's parlance, could only be termed 'a hospital pass': if Judith catches the ball she will do so knowing she may get hurt in the ensuing ruck. Looking down at his fork, Sebastian averts his eyes until he hears Judith speak.

"I find myself asking what Sharon would do in this situation," Judith says.

"What do you mean?" asks Alan. "If Sharon was in what situation?"

"Oh, deciding whether or not go get on the merry-go-round - as Seb so quaintly put it - and then, having done so, how honest she would choose to be."

"That's a bit cryptic," Simon suggests.

Niamh ignores him.

"When did you know ever Sharon to be dishonest?" Niamh protests; then, having heard herself, she backtracks a little. "Occasionally she may have been economical with the truth, I suppose, but never dishonest."

It would be all too easy for Judith to openly settle on the one incident which might have proved the lie to Niamh's statement, but confident each of them can work it out for themselves, she lets it go.

"Maybe I don't mean 'dishonest', but rather - as you suggest - 'economical'. That's a far better word." Judith pauses to take the morsel of de-boned trout into her mouth. When no-one attempts to fill the gap she has deliberately created, she knows it is still 'her turn'. More than that, she is acutely aware that Sebastian - in being open about his relationship with his father - has set the bar high, far higher than Alan and Simon ever could simply because their childhoods had been, in comparison, so unremarkable. Because Sebastian has thrown down the gauntlet, Judith feels she has no choice but to pick it up.

"This feels a little like that dinner-party scene in 'Notting Hill' where they go round the table to see which of them can earn the last brownie. You know the one I mean?" Judith's question is aimed at no-one in particular.

"'That's a pathetic attempt to hog the brownie!' is, I think, the quote," Alan interjects. "Hugh Grant says it to Julia Roberts."

"I love that film," says Niamh; her splitting the final word into two syllables with the 'm' standing alone, remains one of the few traces of her Irish roots.

Sebastian glances at Judith as she lowers her knife to the plate. She has already decided the trout has not been well enough cooked; perhaps she will content herself with picking at the vegetables and then indulge in dessert.

"My attempt at the brownie then," she says, somewhat rhetorically. There is a pause, less for effect than drawing strength, before she fires both barrels. "My mother was an alcoholic." It is an opening which has the desired effect. All eyes are glued to her. "Not that you realise such a thing when you're a child, of course. I suspect not only do children not realise what's going on around them, but they probably don't have the vocabulary to explain it anyway. I recognise the symptoms well enough now, especially given the lifestyle I've led, the things and people I've seen." Wanting to look in Sebastian's direction, instead she forces herself to concentrate on skewering some broccoli. She wonders how far honesty might take her - or how much she should indulge it. "I don't know when it started with her; probably when I was nine or ten. I say that because it must have taken some time for my dad to build up the courage to leave us. He always liked a decent run-up to things; he found being spontaneous difficult - which is an affliction I subsequently decided would never afflict me." She allows another break, partly to nibble at the broccoli and partly in case anyone wants to interject. "I still don't know whether mum's drinking drove him out or something he did turned her to drink; but after he left - I was twelve - her drinking got worse. I don't recall any challenge with money, though obviously we weren't well off. I think she held down a range of fairly menial jobs, each of them for a short period of time. Again I wasn't entirely in tune with her life. I suppose I was struggling with growing up; there are special challenges for young women, aren't there Niamh?" Niamh nods dutifully. "But in a way many of the 'pressures' that came my way - that was the word being used wasn't it? - were the same for me as for the rest of you: who was I? what did I want to do with my life? would I get through the exams? should I go to university and if so, what should I study?" She takes aim at a baton carrot. "So apart from the mother drinking thing, not so different after all."

There is an awkward silence during which Judith's revelation begins to sink in, as they try to judge what she suffered against their own experiences. After a couple of seconds Alan breaks the quiet with a reprise of the 'Notting Hill' quote. The laughter it generates bursts the bubble of the tension which had manifested itself in that brief hiatus.

"But it did make a difference," Niamh observes, "to you I mean. Sharon's experience forced her out of her home; Seb's shaped what he thought he had to do."

"Of course." Judith looks round the table, avoiding Sebastian. "As I said, I was determined not to dither as much as my dad had; so that's one thing. And I guess watching my mum's decline made me more cautious as far as drink was concerned. I don't think I have ever lost control - not in the way she did, anyway. Apart from that? You tell me."

In part, it is a throwaway comment. Each of them, in their own way, seems to consider whether or not Judith is actually asking them to respond, to reveal how they think her childhood is evidenced through the person she has become today. All except for Sebastian.

"You really want to know?"

His delivery - smiling, light-hearted - fails to conceal something of a harder edge, as if he knows he is perfectly capable of making a telling observation and wants to ensure that they - Judith especially - know it too.

Judith laughs.

"I'm not sure you're permitted to answer, Seb."

"Why not?" He pretends hurt. "I'm only trying to defend my pitch for the brownie."

This time the laughter is more general.

"Do I need to tell you why?" Judith asks in turn, her tone perfectly matching his.

"I met Jude's Mum once," he addresses the table before turning to Judith. "Do you remember? That time she came down to visit."

"Were we 'on' or 'off' then? I've lost track."

"I thought she was a lovely woman," Sebastian ignores Judith's sparring. "It was evident that she'd had a rough time of things and wasn't really in control, but it was easy to see how she might have been charming. And she was an attractive woman too - or could have been if she'd have taken the trouble."

"Or if she'd realised it herself," Judith concurs.

"It was easy for me to see where Jude got her looks from." Sebastian smiles at her. "I don't know if you ever noticed it yourself - people so rarely see themselves in their parents." Whether or not he is conscious how this assertion might apply to him, he pauses a fraction of a second to allow the phrase to resonate. "The shape of her face, the mouth, the colour of her hair."

"I didn't realise she'd made such an impression on you, Seb." There is an undertone of sarcasm in Judith's observation.

"She didn't. You did." There is almost an audible gasp from around the table. Sebastian has delivered his words as if they are also a line from a film, stolen perhaps from 'Casablanca' or 'An Affair to Remember'. Alan wishes that he had - at least once in his lifetime - found himself in a position to make such a comment; Niamh, that it had been said by someone to her. Only Simon appears unmoved. Sebastian pushes on. "So you took those things you mentioned from your childhood, and you took your beauty from your mum - whether you want to acknowledge that or not. And I think your early life also gave you a determination to live and explore and embrace variety, adventure. I think it made certain types of people - people most definitely not like your mum and dad, people who were outside the norm - those sorts of individuals became magnets."

"Like you?" Judith laughs, glancing around the table as if seeking support against Sebastian's notion, as if - in a round about way - he is trying to suggest that he is exceptional.

"Why not?"

"I think you flatter yourself, Seb." Focussed solely on him now, it is almost as if the others are absent - or at most, an unpaid audience. "Seeing as you've been complimentary about my looks I'll return the favour. Yes, you are charismatic, handsome in a boyish kind of way. And - even if it's down to your father more than you - there's an aura about you which, I confess, I found attractive. How could I not?" Here Judith takes her eyes from Sebastian and, though she is clearly not seeking any confirmation for her statement, for an instant looks at Niamh. "In fact, you still have some of that charm, that charisma, even if it is a little frayed around the edges. There! I've said it." She laughs at herself.

Sebastian bows his head in mock gratitude.

"You're too kind, Princess."

"But I'm immune now. I was immunised before I left. You saw to that."

"Then I'm as heartbroken now as I was the day you told us you were leaving."

Sebastian's statement is delivered as if merely intended as a joke, perfectly timed to remove any potential poison from what Judith had said - and to elicit a laugh from Niamh and something more grudging from Simon. Yet it is the kind of joke which hides a truth, though exactly how much truth is open to interpretation and preference. Only Sebastian can know whether he was heartbroken or not, and only Judith can know what effect that news - interpreted as true or not - might have on her.

"Bravo."

They all turn toward Alan, his word delivered without fanfare, humour or praise.

"Bravo?" Sebastian is still smiling.

"An accomplished performance, Seb. Very - 'theatrical'." Alan is clearly not being complimentary.

"I'm so glad you liked it."

"I know it was a long time ago - water under the bridge and all that - but I think you can talk only about heartbreak if you know exactly what it feels like." Although it is Alan speaking, Niamh and Judith exchange glances.

"Come on, Alan! We were just kids," Sebastian protests. "Compared to what we've all experienced since, most of what we did back then surely didn't matter, didn't count for much." He glances to Judith and then back to Alan. "Some of it did of course, the important stuff, but we didn't really know what was going on, did we?"

"Some of us still don't." It is unclear to whom Simon is referring other than it is certainly not himself.

"But heartbreak?" The manner in which Alan delivers the word suggests his use of it is loaded with an entirely different meaning in comparison to that uttered by Sebastian, almost as if it were from another vocabulary altogether - if not another language. "Yes, you can say that each of us suffered in our own way - and obviously we did as we were starting to grow up - but 'heartbreak' is such a specific thing."

"And you're an expert on the subject?" Sebastian's smile has faded.

"I know what it feels like, if that's what you mean. Jude may and Niamh may as well - and even you may too, Seb - but back then? Really? And don't forget the reason we're here today. What about Sharon? What state was her heart in at the end of eighty-eight - because I know mine was in pieces…"

One by one they have stopped eating such that, when silence falls, it remains unviolated by the sound of cutlery on china. From nowhere a waiter appears.

"How is everything?" he asks, casting his gaze nervously around the table at diners who are suddenly not eating and have in front of them plates on which - with the exception of Simon's - there is still food.

"Fine, thank you," Niamh offers. "We're just pacing ourselves."

As the waiter retreats, Simon's eyes follow him to the back of the restaurant; the rest look at what remains of their entree as if it has suddenly appeared out of thin air and landed unbidden in front of them. Judith makes the effort to load a little more trout onto her fork and then remembers she had no intention of finishing it, so allows it to slip back to the plate. Niamh and Sebastian resume eating.

"How was she after we all left?" Alan asks, his question aimed at Niamh. "Sharon, I mean."

"How was she?" Niamh takes a moment to try and focus her response. "She was as she always had been I suppose. Sad to see you all go. We both were." She takes a moment to look around the table in order to include them all. "But you know what she was like; she just got on with things. I've rarely seen her ruffled by anything." She laughs to herself. "Can I say that? Is that the opposite of 'unruffled' or should it be something else?"

No-one replies.

"I think that's one of the things I loved about her the most." It is clear Alan feels it's his turn to speak. If Sebastian has knocked them off course, derailed them and taken the focus away from where it should be, then he is duty bound to try and make the correction - as much for himself as for Sharon. He wants to tell them how he had been shattered by Sharon's decision to abandon him, a pain multiplied many-fold thanks to her brief liaison with Sebastian; he wants them to know what he thinks about that episode and - more significantly - what it did to him. In those few weeks he felt his life being hollowed out. *That* was heartbreak. He starts at the beginning. "Of course at first I didn't know what it was; I mean, I didn't think there was anything between us. I can't even remember the sequence of events that made us into a couple."

"Can I say we were surprised?" There is a degree of nervousness in Niamh's voice. "If we're being candid, I mean."

"Why not?" They all glance to Simon, expecting more. He says nothing further.

"And although I didn't know her as well then as I did later - obviously - I was never convinced that she was looking for any romance herself. Not really."

"But there was clearly a trigger." Judith tries to steal a glance at Simon without being noticed. "We're all subject to triggers, aren't we, little things that set us off unexpectedly."

"You make us sound like greyhounds flying out of the traps!"

Although it would have undoubtedly been funny under different circumstances, Sebastian's attempt at levity falls flat.

"Well if we were," Simon's observation is delivered dryly, "then some of our traps failed to open, no matter how hard we tried to get out of them."

"Which just goes to show, doesn't it?"

"Show what Niamh?" Judith seeks clarity on behalf of them all.

"How random everything is. Or can be. Just luck, I guess."

"Well, luck or not," Alan picks up the thread, "she changed me. And for the better, I hope. For the best part of two years I was as happy as I'd ever been." He pauses. "The happiest I ever was. I was in awe of her every day, as if she was a kind of miracle; and from absolutely nowhere I'd had this wonderful gift bestowed on me."

It is a statement - delivered in such an honest way - that seems to disqualify the possibility of any kind of challenge.

"I'm sure she felt the same," Judith tells him, apparently keen to ensure the tone of the conversation is more upbeat. "It can get you like that." If no-one is entirely sure what Judith is referring to when she talks about 'it', most of them can substitute something readily enough in order to make her platitude meaningful to them. "And if it goes away - withers on the vine, if you like - it's all the more sweeter when it returns."

"If that's true, then my education's incomplete," Simon observes.

"In my case it didn't come back." Picking up his glass, Alan looks into what remains of his wine as if it might be the equivalent to a crystal ball, a mirror on the past. "And when it gets taken away - and with it the perfect future you'd started to imagine for yourself - well…"

"Heartbreak." Judith finishes Alan's sentence for him. She looks at Sebastian, her glance loaded. It is a look suggesting not only that he must know what Alan means - after all, Alan has hardly disguised it! - but that his role in the events which played out that summer is central and undeniable.

"She was happy too, Alan," Niamh says, similarly keen to pursue a more favourable course. "Later, after you'd all gone away and enough time had passed, when we talked about those times she always remembered you fondly. I never understood why she didn't try to keep in touch - though that applies to all of us to varying degrees, doesn't it? She once told me that you'd spoiled her."

"Spoiled her?" Alan is incredulous. "How could I have spoiled her? Surely it was the other way round?"

"You'd set the bar too high - that was the phrase she used. Yes, she'd moved on and was already becoming a different person - we'd all moved on, hadn't we? - but if it's any consolation, you shouldn't underestimate the effect you had on her." Keen to corral the conversation, she ropes them all in. "The effect we each had on each other."

For a couple of minutes they fall to eating again as if clearing their plates will allow them to close the topic, though whether it is one recalled as something distasteful or not depends on their individual perspectives. Sebastian feels unusually chastened; Simon resentful to have been excluded from Sharon's affections - and still uncomprehending how she chose Alan over him. If Alan himself has regained a degree of equilibrium then it is largely because of the certainty in Niamh's last affirmation; even if he doesn't quite know what it means, at least it confirms that he mattered.

"How much do you know about Malcolm, Niamh?" As if she is floating above them, pretending to be untouched by the consequences of Sharon's relationships, Judith feels able to move things along. Although she and Sebastian had been uncoupled when he went off the rails, she tells herself his subsequent interactions made no material difference to her at all; surely by that point she had decided she was done with him. "I mean, if we are filling in gaps here, then most of us know so little about him." She glances to Alan who confirms her suspicion with a nod of the head.

"Of course, I forget that none of you ever met Malcolm." Niamh offers a smile as she chastises herself for momentarily misplacing them in time. "It was, what, about ten years later she met him, a couple of years before the millennium. She'd gone to an NHS conference at which they were briefing people about the potential impact January 1st 2000 might have; you know, that thing about the world's computers going haywire, machines ceasing to function, cars becoming uncontrollable or failing to start at all. They wanted people to be prepared. Malcolm worked at one of the big hospitals in Brighton, so not very far away. A technical guy of some kind; I never really did understand what he did. If I'm honest I'd have to say he was a bit of a strange fish; not exactly cold, but more logical than emotional. He never struck me as the romantic type. Actually, he reminded me of..." She shakes her head. "Never mind; I doubt you'd know who I mean." Blushing sightly, she is suddenly flustered. "Where was I?"

"Malcolm wasn't romantic?" Sebastian prompts.

"Oh, yes. Or rather, no. On one level they seemed quite a good match, but on another... You know, I'm not sure there was ever any real affection there - not from her side anyway."

"And yet they married." Alan tries to state the fact as dispassionately as possible, yet they cannot fail to note the sense of loss in his voice. He might as well have said "it should have been me".

"A super-low-key affair. And quick. I was a little surprised myself," Niamh confesses. "But there were other factors at work, I think. Sharon was thirty-eight by then remember; she might have worried about being left on the shelf. And perhaps she thought it was her last chance to have children - not that she'd shown any inclination or interest in them up to that point."

"Maybe it was because of the millennium!"

"You might well joke, Seb, but a lot of people did some pretty strange things around that time. The end of the world was an excuse for just about anything." Niamh pauses in order to relocate herself in her narrative. "So she moved to Brighton and left me in the house on my own. Two years later she was back. There never were any children - though whether that was fate or choice I couldn't find out - and the divorce seemed to go through easily enough. The most she would acknowledge was that Malcom had demonstrated he was 'incompatible', whatever that meant. Fundamentally I think she'd made a mistake and as soon as she realised it she extricated herself. There had been one or two others before Malcolm, but nothing that serious."

"Or that close to the turn of the century."

As if it were a prompt, their laughter at Sebastian's joke is coincident with the arrival of restaurant staff come to remove their plates. For a few moments they go through the pantomime of assuring the waiters that everything was fine - except for Judith who passes comment on the trout - and they then confirm that they would like to see the dessert menu. It is only when these are in hand that Alan speaks.

"And what happened to you during the time Sharon was in Brighton?"

"Me?" Niamh sounds surprised she still has a role to play in the verbal re-enactment of their historical drama.

"Yes. After all, some of the things you said about Sharon could have applied equally well to you. Biological clock ticking and all that."

"Simon!" It is Judith who is angered on Niamh's behalf.

"What?"

"Don't you think that's a little rude?"

"Not really." He defends himself. "It may not be politically correct Jude, but isn't it to the point? Surely if it applied to Sharon then it applied to Niamh…"

"It's fine, it's fine." Fearing Simon is about to tack 'and you too' onto his response to Judith, Niamh dives in. "And Simon's right. How could he not be? I'm sure we've all been through similar moments, each of us. Of course it's different for men, but there must be something akin to a 'biological clock' as far as fatherhood is concerned." Although her supposition is delivered rhetorically, Alan chooses to support her.

"I think you're probably right, Niamh."

"Well I didn't face any such dilemma," Simon says. From his tone it is unclear whether he is boasting or disappointed. "We just had the bloody kids and got it over and done with."

As if it was coordinated, they all look at Sebastian rather than pursue the opening Simon has offered them.

"Don't look at me!" He laughs. "No idea what you're talking about! And if there are any mini-Sebastian's running around, I'm not aware of them."

He delivers his statement with evident insincerity, the last phrase accompanied by an exaggerated wink at Judith, something which once again forces Niamh forward.

"You're right Simon," she says, back into the chain. "Of course I'd thought about children - in fact I'm sure it was a topic Sharon and I discussed on more than one occasion - but by the time she married Malcolm, I think I'd managed to scratch that particular itch. So, when she went off to Brighton nothing much changed for me other than she was no longer here for me to talk to... Although I was happy for her - even if a little sceptical about the whole Malcolm-thing - that didn't stop me feeling a little selfish, a little sorry for myself from time to time."

"Billy-no-mates," Sebastian suggests. Judith shakes her head.

"Yes, Seb, I suppose so, given how long Sharon and I had been sharing a house together." She chooses her words with care. "And again, being alone is probably somewhere each of us has been…"

Niamh is interrupted by the arrival of a waiter brandishing a notepad. They settle on desserts. Judith makes a show of choosing something only after protesting that she really shouldn't, her earlier decision - made on the back of the disappointing trout - remaining her secret.

"Crème brûlée; my favourite!"

Alan and Simon settle on something more robust, Sebastian and Niamh a 'fruits-of-the-forest' cheesecake. When asked about coffee it is Sebastian who asserts "not just yet" and asks for another bottle of wine, something which prompts Judith to count the empties already on the table. Three.

"So your life was quiet, when Sharon was in Brighton?" Alan brings them back.

"Quiet? Ridiculously so, I suppose." Niamh ponders for a moment. "Just a boring routine of work and the kinds of things we all need to do to stay alive; you know, shopping, cleaning, eating. It was dull, but in a way that was fine. I told myself it was nice having some 'me time'."

"But it hadn't always been dull?" Judith concludes.

"With Sharon? No."

"That's not what I meant. When you were talking about children you said that you'd 'scratched that itch' - or something similar. What did you mean?"

Niamh smiles wistfully at Judith. A small sigh escapes. She was always going to have to tell them about James. From the very first moment Judith had crossed the threshold the previous day she'd had a sense that what Sharon had wanted to happen would come to pass: forty-eight hours where no secrets could be safe.

"I nearly beat her to the altar." Had it been acceptable to gasp audibly, Niamh senses that is what she might have heard in response to her statement. As it is, Alan and Judith content themselves with leaning slightly further forward, while Sebastian does the opposite.

"Nearly?" Simon, remaining motionless, is the one who echoes her word.

"And luckily I didn't." Niamh smiles. "Not that's what I thought at the time, obviously."

"When was that?" Judith asks, craving detail. "And why lucky?"

"When?" Niamh makes a minor show of trying to locate the date, as if it isn't there on the tip of her tongue having already made the short journey from were it is etched in her memory. "June ninety-six. We even had a date pencilled in. The 21st."

"The longest day," Simon observes.

"And it probably would have been." Niamh smiles. "And the years after, too. His name was James. He was one of the managers in the hospital and had recently come into HR. His story was that he had been moved as a result of a promotion, that the Trust liked to move senior managers around when they promoted them. It wasn't commonplace, I knew that much, but it did happen."

"They do that in the Army," Alan says.

"And they do it in M&S. Or used to." Everyone glances at Judith. She blushes slightly, guilty that she has intervened. "I used to know someone who worked there."

"Thanks for that Jude," Sebastian's tone is slightly mocking.

"Well James was new and dynamic; he seemed to have fresh ideas, and he shook the place up for a while. I'm not sure if I was most enamoured with him or with what he was trying to achieve. It doesn't matter really. The upshot was that within days I was smitten and within weeks we were going out. Such rapid commitment wasn't usual for me - though to be honest, on the love front there was insufficient romance for anything to be usual." She shares an apologetic smile. "Which probably made me fall the harder, I suppose. After a few months things started to get serious - and I started to make plans. We talked about the future - including June 21st - and I thought I could see my life mapped out."

"And Sharon?"

"Sharon?" Niamh looks at Alan. She shakes her head so subtly they almost miss the gesture. "Sharon was - well, Sharon. She didn't know James personally, but she'd heard about him. He had a reputation, shall we say. So she challenged me, gently of course; wanted to know what I felt, if I was sure. I saw later that she was trying to help, to influence, but without being too intrusive or brazen about it. I mean, she could have been brutal and told me what she'd heard, what she really thought - but she could see what that might potentially do to our friendship."

"You'd have to choose," Judith deduces.

"Probably. Between her and James, yes. And she could see how 'all-in' I was and I guess she didn't want to risk losing me. It must have been difficult for her…" Niamh nods as Sebastian offers to refill her wine glass. "When I started to hear the rumours myself, that gave her permission to be slightly more forthright."

"Rumours?" Sebastian smiles as if he understands all too well. "There are always rumours."

"A junior doctor in Radiography; a senior nurse on one of the orthopaedic wards."

"No smoke without fire?" Alan concludes on behalf of them all.

"A complete blaze, as it turned out." There is something in the laugh Niamh lets slip that betrays both how hard that time had been for her and how fortunate she now realises she was to escape from it. "Once it was obvious I had no future with him - unless I wanted to be just a token wife, one of many almost - Sharon came into her own. Ninety-six wasn't an easy year; I can't pretend otherwise. During that time Sharon was more than a friend. She was my support, my counsellor, my confidant; she kept me sane, on the straight-and-narrow. I suppose I became something of a project for her. To be rescued. When Malcolm appeared on the scene I was just about cured - which left her free to do what she did."

"Your experience didn't put her off?" Simon asks somewhat indelicately. It is a question that draws a frown from Judith.

"In a way almost the opposite. I think it was one of the things that made her realise the clock was ticking. Part of her wanted a shot at the Holy Grail - if that's what it was - even if it ended badly. Which it did, obviously."

"The Holy Grail?" Judith laughs. "If that's what marriage is then heaven help us!"

Sebastian reaches for the fresh bottle of wine a waiter has just deposited on the table.

"From what you said earlier, I expect you'd agree with that wouldn't you Simon, about marriage not being the Holy Grail?" Sebastian smiles, attempting to be conspiratorial. "Representing the male side of the equation, if you like. 'Bloody kids' and all that. Alan and I can't comment - at least not from an insider's perspective. And isn't there a joke about marriage being 'an institution' - like a madhouse?!"

"But don't you think it's odd," Niamh intercepts before Simon can respond, "that of the five of us, only Simon is married? Surely that's unusual."

"Statistically speaking, I'm sure it is," says Alan. "If we were representative of a normal distribution I would expect three of us to be married - possibly one of whom would be in a same sex relationship - then one divorced, and the other…"

"I think we'd always be in the 'other' camp, don't you Jude?" Sebastian laughs. Judith smiles grudgingly.

"So I'm the odd one out," Simon pulls them back, "because I'm normal?"

"'Normal'? Surely 'conventional'." The correction comes from Alan - which clearly surprises one or two of them. "I mean, married with two kids. And what is 'normal' anyway?"

His observation has a downbeat tone to it, a track from which - fearing they will suddenly sag into a miasma of philosophy - Sebastian immediately feels the need to elevate them.

"So Simon, given none of us have a Scooby Doo, what's it like being married, a father, a pillar of the suburban community? Describe the journey to becoming 'Commuter Man'."

No-one finds Sebastian's portrait particularly funny, especially not Simon whose face has remained stoney throughout.

"It depends on your perspective, Seb. Clearly for you the whole scenario is utterly ridiculous. How can you possibly comprehend any of it, anyway?"

"You might be surprised." They look at Judith, not having expected her to respond. A cloud passes over Sebastian's face. She glances at him and then back to Simon. "How did you meet her? Your wife, I mean. Maybe start there."

"Dawn?" Having been thrown off track by Sebastian, Simon takes a moment to reorientate himself. "At a training-cum-conference event. We were working for different companies but in the same line of business. Although it was a random assignment, they'd placed us on the same table and in the same group for the practicals - you know, role-play stuff. We'd joked about how we couldn't talk about our work because of competition law. It went from there."

"No fireworks?"

"No, Seb; not that I can remember. It was all perfectly - normal." He emphasises the word. "We arranged to meet a week or so later; then we met again. It just happened. I didn't think about it, or plan it. And when we got as far as marriage, well that's seemed the right thing to do too."

Not being sure how to respond, they are rescued by the arrival of desserts. The soft clatter of cutlery on crockery begins again.

"And what are you children called?" Niamh picks up the thread.

"Jonathan's the eldest. He's not long finished at Sheffield Hallam where he studied physics and chemistry. He wants to work somewhere glamorous like CERN, but for now he's at an ex-ICI plant based in the North East. And Gwen - it was Dawn's late mother's name - is working hard to get her grades so that she can read English at Bristol."

"What does she want to do afterwards?" Alan takes his turn, knowing somewhere close to the surface there is a joke about being able to read English anywhere - and that Sebastian, beginning to show signs of the wine catching up with him, may be just about to crack it.

"She has no idea - which I suppose is okay for now. But what can you do with an English degree except teach?" He leaves the question hanging, half-expecting someone to pick up on it and challenge him. But it is too old a notion to excite anyone.

"So soon you and Dawn will be footloose and fancy free." Robbed of a chance to be overtly funny, Sebastian delivers his question as a statement which - given he is talking about Simon - is laced with irony.

"I wouldn't say that exactly." Simon takes the question at face value. "We won't be totally liberated until Gwen's finished at Bristol and gone off to work. But now? Since Jonathan left? Dawn probably feels it more than I do. The seven-fifteen from Bexhill still leaves at seven-fifteen, and I still need to be on it."

Before he can say anything, Niamh looks at Sebastian in such a way as to prevent his reiteration of the 'Commuter Man' gag. She further ensures his silence by jumping in herself.

"And after that? Any plans?" As soon as she has asked, Niamh regrets her oversight. Their conversation on the walk back from the cemetery comes to her. With the outcome of his tests hanging over him, how can Simon make any plans? She tries to offer an apology in the way she looks at him, trying in the slight frown that flickers across her face to demonstrate she is chastising herself.

"Not really." There is no indication in Simon's voice that he has registered the subtlety in Niamh's expression. "Mind you, I've never been a big one for plans, not really. Things just happen, don't they? There's your routine - I'm sure we all have our routines - and we fit things around those as best we can. Is there much space for anything else? Really? For the majority of us, I suspect not." He looks down at his sticky toffee pudding accusingly, as if it represents the physical manifestation of his restraints. Here is something else he has to do, to eat, to endure; part of the pantomime in which he is trapped. Yet eat he still does, dutifully plunging his spoon into the sponge's surface because he has no idea what the alternative might look like.

"Well I'm pretty sure I know at least one person who's not tied down to anything as dull and boring as a routine." They look up from their desserts as Sebastian, pausing for effect, attempts to load his fork with another chunk of cheesecake.

"You obviously mean me, don't you Seb?"

Sebastian looks up.

"Who else, Jude dearest?" When he offers her his most complete smile, the one that seems to blend friendship, caring, comradeship, boyish bonhomie - and not a little sexy menace - both she and Niamh recognise traces of the Sebastian he used to be.

"Because I don't have a 'normal' job?"

"Because your 'job' is so ridiculously un-normal!" He laughs. "And because of where it has taken you, the people you have met, the things you have done." There is a pause before the last phrase which is fractionally longer than it needed to be, the gap laden with all the things his smile doesn't convey. Sebastian assumes the posture of a lawyer addressing a jury. "Don't be seduced by the notion that my learned friend's life is all excitement and glamour. Not a bit of it. I put it to you that she has paid a high price for the life she leads. Surely you will agree with me that she is as much a victim as anything else - and on that basis I demand that you acquit her of these unfounded charges!" The final statement is delivered with expansive hand gestures which result in a morsel of cheesecake separating itself from Sebastian's fork and falling to the table.

"Ooops."

Only Niamh hears Simon's comment.

"Well for once you're right, Seb. 'All excitement and glamour'?" As she glances around the restaurant, drab in its provinciality, Judith cannot help but recall some of the other restaurants she has patronised: New York, Sydney, Paris, Capri, Stockholm. There had certainly been excitement and glamour in some of those, for sure. "As you say, that's not the whole story."

"Though it *is* exciting?" It is as if Niamh wishes to get at least one of the threads of her friend's life pinned down.

"Formula 1 at Monaco, the Derby - even the Oscars, for God's sake! How can that not be exciting?" Alan offers evidence for the prosecution.

"Ah yes," before Judith can respond, Sebastian interjects, doing so in such as way as to prevent them from deducing on which side of the argument he has chosen to settle. "But Jude is there not on her own account, not really; she is at those things because someone else needs to be there: Marco Whats-his-name, the ex-racing driver; or that Paolo guy, the film director. That's what I meant."

"'What you meant'?" Now it is Judith's turn to try and gain a firm foothold.

"About the price you have to pay."

Implicit in Sebastian's statement is the proposition that she has to sacrifice something of herself in order to enjoy such global events. It is a statement which could be interpreted as recognition that all the excitement and glamour comes at a cost most people do not appreciate. Alongside of his apparent defence of her, his words suggesting she is merely a pawn in that world, it is clear that beneath their surface Sebastian could be saying something else entirely.

Judith smiles.

"As usual, you're being far too dramatic - though there *is* a world of difference between what people see and what they don't see. At least you've got that part right."

"What don't we see?" Simon asks.

"Everything that goes on behind those fashion shoots, for example. What's made available for public consumption - the ad, the poster, the photograph - is just the end product, the tip of an iceberg. No-one sees the work that goes into producing those things: the hours of discomfort, the boredom, the monotony - and sometimes the pain."

"The pain?" The tone in Niamh's voice suggests an equation she cannot resolve.

"I once did a shoot for lingerie in Finland. They wanted to contrast the colours of the underwear - scarlet, black - with the brilliant white of the snow and the vastness of the landscape. It was something to do with suggesting the kit made you hot, made you stand out from the crowd. I don't know. Anyway, it was absolutely freezing! We were there for hours and, in spite of the heavy coats and blankets, I got *so* cold. I felt frost-bitten everywhere."

"Everywhere?" Sebastian asks playfully. Judith ignores him.

"But no-one saw any of that. They never do. I think it was easier in the early days - easier for me, I mean - because I was younger, keen, desperate, prepared to do anything, to put up with whatever was necessary in order to get my career going. These days... Well, that kind of thing is a little harder. And along with that, the game's changed."

"Now they just need you to model bobble hats and slippers!" This time they all laugh - including Judith.

"Seb, you absolute bastard!" she says.

"But Seb's right isn't he? At least partly?" Niamh pauses as Judith looks her way. "I mean, they want you to do different things now, don't they? Different sorts of fashion, for example. And that thing you did on TV - you know, the small piece on that travel show. Wasn't that great! And aren't those things, all that variety, a natural progression in your career?"

"I'm getting older, you mean? Can't cut it with the young kids any more."

"That's not what Niamh said, Jude." Alan leaps into the breach.

"No I know she didn't," Judith is still smiling, "at least not in so many words. But you're right, Niamh. Of course I'm getting older, and of course I have to pursue different assignments and am asked to do different things. But I'm still in the game, and that's what counts."

Although it is a phrase delivered lightly, there is a resonance about her last statement that is not lost on any of them.

"And it's wonderful that you still are."

That these words are spoken by Sebastian takes them a little by surprise, none more so than Judith herself. They look at him as he smiles a little blearily before taking his glass to his lips once more - and then it's as if a taste of the wine flips a switch.

"But that isn't what I meant about Monaco or the Oscars, though. You weren't there on a shoot or to promote a product or because someone had paid you to be. You were there to be seen - or wanting to be seen. None of that was work, was it? Oh, I realise those adventures came about because their foundations were the photoshoots and ads and magazines, and because you are stunning and gorgeous and all that, but they were something else weren't they, Jude? They were personal choices."

"No-one just *chooses* to go the the Oscars, Seb!" Judith laughs as if it is the most ridiculous thing she has ever heard.

"Don't you have to be invited?" Niamh's question could hardly be more innocent.

"Yes, of course you do," Judith confirms.

"But you have to be 'in the business', a member of the Academy or whatever it's called. So Jude's right, you can't just rock-up." If they are confused by Sebastian's argument, one which seems to be weaving to and fro, he continues to pursue its thread. "If you're not then you need to know someone who's going to be invited - like that Paolo chap. And you can't just wander into the pit lane at Monaco; you have to be invited, attached…"

The smile she had been wearing so confidently for most of the last few minutes has begun to leave Judith's face. The innuendo in Sebastian's words suggests he is trying to uncover a different truth. Although keeping the focus on the 'public' Judith, the persona she exposes to everyone, his preoccupation is clearly not with her career and what she has achieved there. He is trying to draw a hard line between public and private, and it is the latter he is stalking. If Judith detects a trace of bitterness, of defiance in his tone, it is one which reminds her of some of their final fights, of the unsavoury side of him.

"What are you getting at, Seb?" Knowing she cannot back down, that she must demonstrate her superiority over him, Judith's question - and the manner in which she delivers it - casts a sudden shadow across the table. The other three realise that, if a storm is coming, they will need to ride it out.

"Me? Nothing really. I'm just making an observation, I suppose."

"Which is?" Sebastian having taken her this far, Judith has decided she is not going to let him wriggle out of admitting what's on his mind.

"That your adventures - you know, everything that gets into the papers these days, like Monaco and the rest of it - come about thanks to the men in your life. Glitz and glamour, flashbulbs and soundbites. I can't help but believe that on one level it's - I don't know - phoney, fake. Not your career, obviously, but an offshoot of it, a byproduct if you like. And yet simultaneously I also wonder whether the spin-offs happen by accident or even by default; whether your relationships - Marco, that Swedish Count, the Scottish Laird, the oil magnate's son from Texas, etcetera - were ones you somehow inadvertently and unavoidably found yourself in. Or whether they were deliberately cultivated. 'Friends with benefits'. Because one way or another, Jude, your life must have been - must be - one hell of a rollercoaster, the implications of which us mere mortals don't actually get to see. That's what I meant by the price you'd had to pay."

If Sebastian intended his conclusion to close out his thesis, it proves to be merely the calm; the rumble of thunder comes in Judith's next question.

"Are you accusing me of being some kind of tart, Seb, because if you are then I have to say that's a bit rich coming from you!"

Sebastian tries a smile, as if that will be sufficient to pour oil on troubled waters. He leans forward for the only bottle with wine remaining in it and refills his glass; then he raises the bottle to the light to check how much is left.

"I'm just trying to understand what your life is like. I'm trying to reconcile how the person I see today - who we all see in those tabloid photos or news clips - has migrated from modelling and advertisements, catalogues and posters, to being someone else, someone 'public' to be consumed by the masses. I'm simply trying to understand what the cost has been for you - and what choices you made (or didn't make) along the way in order to get there."

"Why? Why the hell should you care?"

"I care, Jude, because I used to care. I used to care very much."

Whether he had intended it as such or not, Sebastian's statement is delivered as if it is yet another stolen from an Oscar-bound film. Perhaps it was premeditated - or perhaps it's simply the result of his having had sufficient wine to loosen his tongue, already too many glasses to have kept track. Its effect - other than to quell any danger of the storm worsening - is to steal the wind from Judith's sails, as if his words have managed to both negate her anger and confess his past feelings in one fell swoop. That he has not withdrawn his challenge, leaving it extant and unanswered, is certainly not lost on Niamh, nor potentially Alan; but Judith is suitably unsettled as to find her wrath diminished to almost nothing.

"There are lots of other things, peripheral and private, people don't see - in addition to all the background hard work I mentioned earlier." Judith's tone is one of reminiscence. There is a blend of regret and melancholy about it, almost as if she were keen to expand upon the role of victim Sebastian had posited a little while earlier. "I think I was prepared for the work when I started out, even though I could have had no real comprehension of what would be involved. But what I couldn't possibly have known was how my life would change. I don't mean the photos or the magazines or how I was suddenly 'visible'; but rather what all of that made me."

"What it made you?" Unexpectedly Alan finds himself drawn in to Judith's narrative, almost as if she is about to reveal the secret of a puzzle he has been trying to solve.

"Yes. Being visible turned me into a kind of commodity, I suppose; so very different from how I'd been when I lived here with you." She glances round the table ensuring she connects with each of them. "We lived on equal terms with each other; we were our own people, weren't we? But once I gained a degree of … I don't know what the right word is - except it isn't 'fame'… Whatever. Anyway, without realising it at some point I became public property and started to move in different circles. Perhaps people wanted to see if the reality matched their fantasy; perhaps they just wanted to have someone decorative at their parties. It happened to most of the girls, invitations to events, openings, premieres, shows. Don't get me wrong; it was thrilling, affirming, proof that you'd 'arrived' and were a success. Even as someone in their mid- to late-twenties I confess to having been naïve about all of that. I've no idea how some of the younger girls managed. A lot didn't. And I suppose I was also naïve about the people I met at parties and the other things. Many were there for a common reason, a shared motivation: to be seen, to keep their profile up. Image was everything, and keeping your image visible, in the public eye, was critical. Disappear off the radar for too long and you might as well be dead. For some … well, they were gifted opportunities to go trophy hunting; particularly men of a certain age. Having a glamorous young lady at your party was one thing, but having her on your arm was something else entirely!"

"Or in your bed."

"But you still had a choice? I mean, in terms of where you went, what you did."

Ignoring Sebastian's crude observation, Judith looks to respond to Niamh.

"You'd like to think so, wouldn't you? But sometimes that wasn't the case - especially when it came to where you went. Everyone had an angle of some kind, and often the agency or the magazine asked us to be at party A or premiere B in order to sweeten some deal or other."

"And once you were there?" Sebastian resurrects his question, though in calmer waters now.

"You couldn't help but be flattered, Seb. Suddenly there would be this famous actor or musician who made a pass or offered you a trip to Monte Carlo or Nice or Rome. It was intoxicating, often irresistible. I suppose I was drunk on it for a while." She looks at him. "Maybe it was as if I was addicted - which, as you may know - is a hard gig to turn down."

"And did you turn it down?" Although he feels he knows the answer, Sebastian wants to give Judith the opportunity to complete her confession. She smiles wistfully.

"Not as often as I should have, as I'm sure you'll have deduced - especially based on some of the 'red top' coverage over the years… Unsurprisingly, not all of it has been accurate."

"Or fair," Niamh offers.

"Indeed." Judith pauses as if she is unsure how close she is to finishing her story. "The tabloids can be very - fickle. Often what they cover and how they cover it depends on what else is in the news, what other celebrities may or may not have done."

"Or what you did yourself?"

Judith smiles at Sebastian, her confidence returning, believing she has regained control. The ground feels solid enough for her to give him a little of what he craves.

"Sometimes, yes. But it was all luck in a way - both good and bad. In terms of the coverage you got, I mean. Or didn't get. There were one or two of my relationships they liked to feast on; not because of me, you understand, but because of Marco or Bryan. They were celebrities in their own right; perhaps fading ones, but good copy nonetheless." She weighs up her last move. "Did I make some mistakes along the way? Yes, of course I did. And I know that's what you want to hear Seb, and it's true. For a while my life was a little like a conveyor belt - mainly in terms of work, but not entirely. You lose the ability to be discerning, to make good decisions. One or two of my former beaux were anything but that!" She laughs, then catching the eye of a nearby waiter, waves him over. "Shall we get another bottle before we order coffee?"

The question is to the table but her eyes are on the young man now at her side. She knows he has recognised her; there is an undeniable 'tell' men cannot help but offer. Once upon a time she would have wanted to find out the source of the recognition - which campaign, which article, which photograph - but these days acknowledgement itself is sufficient. She remembers the drive-thru Starbucks.

The others watch as she slips effortlessly into her working persona, teasing the waiter with just a little of her 'celebrity magic'. It is a trick that has often been rewarded with better service, faster passage through airports, room upgrades in hotels. For many on the receiving end, being graced with a smile or a wink is enough; for others - the more business-minded - recognising that such celebrity can rub off on them, they know they need to make the most of even the thinnest of acquaintance, and that a modest endorsement might just boost trade. As the waiter walks away from their table carrying three empty bottles, Judith looks back to find them all smiling at her.

"What?" At least part of her enquiry is genuine.

"You know I've never understood how any of that works." Alan looks away from her and down to his empty glass which he chooses to leave unfilled. Judith waits for him to return his gaze to her. "Celebrity, I mean. I see people on tv and such like and it seems that many of them are living in a rarified atmosphere denied to mere mortals like me, and that the world they inhabit is totally unreal. I'm not saying that's you, Jude - " he rushes on to plug the gap, "but you do know what I mean? Surely there are some people even you can't believe?"

"Are there different levels of insanity? I think that's what Alan wants to know."

Turning to Simon, Judith wants to laugh at his attempted clarification but is unable to do so. Alan's question has made her wonder how they may view her, the Judith she is today, not the one from years gone by. And in a way it is a query which is reflexive, forcing her to ask the same questions of herself: where is she on the spectrum of 'insanity' Simon has posited, and what does she actually see when she looks in the mirror in the morning? Any sense of control and security she may have been rebuilding over the previous few minutes simply evaporates.

A brief silence, broken only by a faint backing-track of soft chatter and the clinking of cutlery and glasses from elsewhere, tells her they expect an answer. There is a burst of laughter from an unseen table.

"I do know what you mean, Alan, and on that basis also how you cannot but fail to understand the 'celebrity world' - nor fail to ask the question you have." Hoping her adoption of implied apostrophes will have gifted her a little distance from the pantomime about which they are speaking, she looks down to where her right hand has started playing with a spoon. Did she give it permission to do that? She drops it to the table. "There are some people who are like that, living in an unreal world as you put it. After a while they become caricatures of themselves. I could mention a few names and you'd all nod your heads agreeing they're sad, or deluded, or whatever. None of your judgements would be positive, right? But it's almost never that simple. Some of them are logical and calculating, perfectly cognisant of what they're doing and why they're doing it. They go over-the-top because over-the-top is good, over-the-top sells, it keeps them in the public eye, relevant."

"Relevant?" Sebastian's surprise at the word is evident.

"In their eyes, yes." Again a slight pause. "And then there are those who lose their way and don't realise the mess they're in. I suppose they're the real victims - especially when people take advantage of them."

"Can't they see it - the mess they're in, the life they're leading?"

"Many can't, Niamh. Again, I could mention some names… You might be surprised. It's just that some people aren't very bright, of course. Not intellectually - though that too - but rather unable to function adequately or responsibly in the world they have come to inhabit, a world capable of outwitting them at every turn. And many are hooked; on the fame and the glamour and the glitz. Some get hooked on other, less savoury things…"

"Drugs?"

"It's one of the problems, Alan, no question. I'm not saying there are huge numbers of people, but some; a proportion."

"And you, Jude?"

A flicker of alarm crosses Judith's face in response to Sebastian's question. Her tone hardens.

"I don't do drugs, Seb. Give me some credit, for Christ's sake!"

"I didn't mean that." There is enough in the tone of his apology for it to ring true. "That spectrum you talked about; you know the calculating egotist who will do anything to get in the paper, through to those who are the victims of the system, the lifestyle. Where are you on that?"

"You think you have to ask?"

"Don't get me wrong," Sebastian tries to placate her, "I don't have you in either camp. How could I? But I don't know, not really. We haven't seen you for so long, any of us. And all we *have* seen of you - until today, that is - is what's fed to us. It's impossible not to build up some kind of picture… I suppose it's about reconciling that with the Jude we knew, the things you said about making choices or falling into things, about being calculating or being a victim… If I'm honest I'd put you in the middle somewhere - because you're too intelligent to be a total victim and not deluded or self-centred enough to be a total arse-wipe."

"You're too generous, Seb." Judith's tone betrays her belief that he is, in fact, being the complete opposite.

"But the middle's a pretty wide expanse," he goes on, failing to accurately interpret what she has said, "certainly big enough to get lost in."

"Sharon always thought you'd be successful." Niamh's observation takes them by surprise, as much in the softness of her tone as the words she has uttered.

"Sharon?" Relieved to be off the treadmill to which Sebastian seemed intent to fix her, Judith welcomes a little diversion - especially if it is going to be a positive one.

"Do you remember your leaving 'do'? Where did we have it again?"

"Wasn't it 'The Royal Oak'?" Alan answers Niamh's question.

"They had that little room out the back with the table football in it."
Sebastian is suddenly animated. "It was always freezing in there."

"And if I remember correctly, you three spent most of the evening in
there." Judith tries to sound hurt.

"I loved that little room," Sebastian says somewhat wistfully.

"It was too close to the toilets and always smelled of piss!" They
laugh at Judith's observation, sensing a little air being let out of the
balloon that might have been in danger of bursting. She turns to
Niamh. "So what did Sharon say? I don't remember anything."

"No, it was a little while later; actually after you'd left. We were
sitting in front of the tv one evening. There must have been
something on the box that triggered her, you know, to think about
you. I've no idea what it could have been. Maybe something on the
news. Anyway, she suddenly said 'You know, Niamh, I think Jude
will do very well'. Just like that; those exact words."

Smiling, Judith wants to feel flattered, vindicated, but somehow she
doesn't feel she has sufficient collateral to be able to do so.

"Why did she think that, Niamh? I mean, it's nice she said it - that
she had that confidence in me - but what was her reasoning? Do
you know?"

Niamh shakes her head.

"I don't. I'm not even sure she justified her comment." She makes a
small show of trying to recall something, anything. "It couldn't have
been because of how you looked, obviously; I don't think any of us
had any doubts on that front." Knowing they still won't have,
Niamh allows Judith a moment to look at the three men to see if
anyone is going to offer a contradictory opinion. "So it must have
been about how you were, I suppose. You know, intelligent, mature
- stuff like that."

"She was always a good judge," says Alan, not simply out of loyalty
but happy to make an endorsement that can only reflect well on him

too. "On that basis - and considering what we've just talked about - I suspect she would never have put you in the victim camp."

"Which is reassuring," Judith says, keeping it brief in order to try and close down the subject.

"Didn't we get completely pissed that night?" Sebastian looks round the table. "All of us, I mean?"

"You were always pissed, Seb," Judith offers with a laugh.

"Though Sharon and I certainly tended not to." Niamh defends herself and her friend. "Not that we didn't, on occasion…"

"We played some kind of tournament on that football table." Sebastian ignores them. "The three of us. Went on for ages. Didn't I win? I think I remember winning; whipping your sorry arses."

"You always won, Seb." There is a note of resignation in Alan's voice, not because he lost at table football, but because Sebastian's claim had been something of a constant refrain during their time together. Even not having heard it for thirty years, it resonates with him instantly.

"I could never get the hang of it," Simon confesses. "Didn't have the wrists for it."

Out of proportion, the laugh that explodes from Sebastian takes them by surprise; it is a laugh fed not only by memories of past events, but by personal prejudice. Whether he intends to or not, Sebastian is making a statement - one he chooses not to endorse with words.

"Maybe it's one of those insignificant examples of how much we've changed. How quickly we changed." With the exception of Sebastian whose eyes are glued to something on the tablecloth, they all look at Simon. "I mean, after that night in 'The Royal Oak' - or after the last time we were all in there together - did any of us ever play table football again?" He pauses to allow someone to answer in the affirmative, but nothing is said. "There you go; just as I thought."

"What do you mean?"

"When we left we moved on, Alan. Just that. And quickly too. Jude to her new career, then Seb, then you and I. And as soon as we were away into new jobs in new places - our new lives - we were immediately different people. Don't you think that?" Simon gives Alan the opportunity to endorse his theory, but again he says nothing. "You'll back me up on this, Jude. Weren't you suddenly a different person as soon as you were in London? Based on what you've already said you must have been…"

"I'm not sure about 'suddenly', but I suppose you're right. Isn't that inevitable though? I mean, Sharon and Niamh didn't go anywhere, but that didn't stop them from becoming different people, did it?"

"You think I've changed?" Niamh asks.

"Of course! Haven't we all? Maybe there's a question of degree, or how fast things happened… Wouldn't it be dreadful if we were still living the same lives now as we had been back then?"

"But - " unnoticed, Sebastian had gradually raised his head and is now looking at Judith once again, "it's not just that, is it? Back then we were living the same *kind* of life, doing similar things, pursuing parallel goals. Afterwards we didn't just change, first we diverged. And to different degrees."

"Explain." Judith cannot resist picking up the thread.

"Niamh may have changed as a person since those 'heady days', but the life she leads now - if you forgive her that big James-shaped bump in the road - is still pretty much on a par. Is that fair, Niamh?" Niamh's nod allows Sebastian to carry on. "Obviously I'm guessing, but I suspect that's likely to be the case for Alan and Simon too - if you ignore Simon's family thing, of course. They may have changed in terms of getting older - and that applies to us all - but their *lives* are not that different. Does that make sense? But for you -"

"Not me again!" pleads Judith. "Isn't it someone else's turn?"

Sebastian overrides her objection.

"But for you, your *life* is as radically different now as you are a person. The life you lead has changed who you are. The two go hand-in-hand; you couldn't have success in your career without allowing yourself to be moulded to fit. Alan's already said that he has never understood the celebrity thing - and how could he? Or Niamh? Or Simon? It's not something which has touched them in any material way, or forced them to become someone else."

"And what about you, Seb?" Judith tries to divert attention away from herself and go on the offensive. "Surely your life is different too?"

"Do you mean because of my dad?"

Judith nods.

Sebastian smiles triumphantly. "Ah, but there you're wrong. You forget I'd always grown up with that kind of 'celebrity' in my life, so there's nothing new at all in that department."

"I'm with Alan," Simon's interruption sounds a little like a reluctant confession. "Not only do I also not understand celebrity and what its component parts are, I'm bothered by the fact that it seems - dishonest." Simon makes a show of searching for the word, yet it leaves his mouth as if he has had it ready and waiting for the last twenty minutes.

"How so?" Although not wanting to seem as if she has taken offence, there is no hiding the air of defensiveness in Judith's voice.

"You said it yourself, Jude. All those examples of people being at events, doing things for ulterior motives; the pursuit of - whatever it is they're after. None of that seems particularly natural, does it? And from what I can see lots of people - women especially, I have to say - are happy to embrace any means of embellishment they can lay their hands on to stand out from the crowd."

"Bigger boobs," Sebastian suggests.

"Mentioning no names," says Simon.

"Kim Kardashian's arse." Sebastian immediately offers a name. There is a ripple of laughter. "Allegedly."

"And all this 'reality tv' crap," Simon is warming to his theme. "Where's the reality in plastic people 'acting' in fake situations, their make-up three feet thick to go with their perfect teeth and perfect tans and perfect bodies?"

"I'm not saying you're wrong, Simon," there is an edge in Judith's voice, "but it's not just women. You forget, I've seen some of the sorts of people you're talking about close up. There's often as much fakery in the men - hair dye, fake tans, muscles that have been supplemented by God-knows-what..."

"Were you ever tempted, Jude?" Niamh's question may be one which has crossed all their minds in the last minute or so.

"What, for fake muscles and a six-pack?"

Sebastian's joke is well aimed; they all laugh just as another bottle of wine arrives, the waiter casting a glance in Judith's direction.

"You know what I mean!" Niamh pretends to be affronted.

"Were you ever approached by someone suggesting a little 'enhancement'? Some 'touching up' here and there?"

"Did you think I needed it, Simon?" Judith defies him to answer her in the wrong way - then heaps on the pressure. "Or that I should be considering something now?"

"No-one's suggesting any such thing," says Sebastian, flipping back into White Knight mode. "How could they? But Simon's point is well made; you know, about the fakery inherent in the trade and the fact that some people will go to any lengths to remain in the limelight."

If he is drawing a thread between this notion and some of the comments he made earlier about Judith's lifestyle, he does so unconsciously. Indeed, it is of such fine twine, gossamer-like, that it remains almost invisible. If any of them do make the connection, they don't show it.

"Fair enough." Judith gives both the fashion for 'enhancement' and the notion of celebrity's 'dishonesty' a moment's thought. The first is easy enough to address, but the second? "You're right, Simon. There are too many people who succumb to the knife or the needle in order to pursue their dreams, their 'fifteen minutes of fame'. And in lots of cases it *is* shallow - and if that means it's dishonest too… But I do know one or two stars, National Treasures who, if I told you they'd also given in to pressure and had 'work done' - well, you'd be astounded."

"Who's that, Jude?" Niamh asks.

Judith laughs.

"But for some of the people you're talking about - and please don't think they're in the majority - I would be inclined to agree that they too don't really understand what celebrity is all about. Not really. And yes, I have been approached on a small number of occasions with 'suggestions' - and no, I've never indulged. Nor would I. Again, some credit please!" She takes a sip of wine. "But dishonest? I don't know; it depends on your definition. If someone is open about having a boob job and the reasons for doing so, is that dishonest? Aren't all those things choices made to try and achieve a goal. Perhaps the subtlety is in the differentiation between the means and the end."

"Tools of the trade?" suggests Alan.

"For some trades," Sebastian suggests with a wink; but this is a joke that generates little laughter.

In the brief lull which follows, Judith finds she cannot divorce herself from dishonesty as much as she would wish to - nor of wanting to measure herself, her life, against something less tainted by external influence. She glances round the table. Is her life any less honest than anyone else's? It is obviously in her best interests to answer in the negative, and yet she is only too well aware there have been times when she has strayed. She may not have been injected with Botox in order to stay up with the pace, but there are many other options open to attractive women, both the young and not so young. As her glance falls on Sebastian, she is suddenly struck by the bizarre notion that her relationship with him - wild, tempestuous, ultimately unrewarding - may have been the most 'honest' thing in her life. Chilled by the thought, she gives herself a mental shake and drains her wine. As she replaces the glass on the table, Sebastian is there, ready with the new bottle to refresh it.

"Celebrity is it's own drug". That's what she wished she had said, but now she fears it is too late, the moment for having done so long since gone. And anyway, it is a stone she has no wish to have turned over once again.

"You realise," she finds herself saying, "that a lot of the sorts of people you're talking about - and I'm generalising here, but I concede they're mainly women - are scared. That's why they resort to plastic and needles and fakery."

"Scared? Of what?" Once again the naïve question - but the one that needs to be asked - comes from Niamh.

"Growing old, losing their looks, finding themselves unable to cut it, being discarded. I've seen some people completely crumble when they realise they no longer have any value as 'public material' and that no-one wants them. It's not just fifteen minutes of fame. Once you've had fifteen, then you want sixteen, then seventeen. But there inevitably comes a point when that extra minute lies just out of reach."

"And does that scare you, Jude?"

Judith smiles, strangely grateful it is Sebastian who has asked the question. Having invested in her in the past, his concern - because it does sound like concern - is all the more meaningful.

"Of course." Her immediate honesty surprises her and she lets a little laugh escape. Beyond anything else, it is finding herself alone which petrifies her more than losing her looks - yet she knows such a confession, here and now, would be taking honesty a step too far. "But aren't we all afraid of something? Deep down, we must be." The smile she offers the table is not one of empathy or encouragement, but of relief; relief that she has finally found a way out of the cross-examination she has been suffering for too long now. "Niamh, what about you?"

"Me?"

"Yes. What are you scared of?"

"I don't know. It's not something I've ever thought about."

"Well think about it now," Sebastian smiles, picking up the bottle again and pouring a little into Niamh's glass. "Here, this will help."

"I doubt it." Niamh lifts it almost immediately and sips the cool white wine. She doesn't take much, just enough to buy her a little thinking time; she knows she has to say something. "I suppose I'm afraid of what most people are scared of: getting old, having bits of me fail or fall off, dying."

"Ah, but none of that counts," Sebastian protests, reenergised by the theme. "That applies to all of us - Jude's just said as much. We can't let you cop out as easily as that." They all laugh softly. "There has to be something *you* are scared of, a thing that applies specifically to you. What are the skeletons in Niamh's cupboard she hopes will never fall out?"

"Now you're just being fanciful," Judith admonishes him, then returns to Niamh. "But he's right, in a way."

What should she say? As Niamh juggles to articulate a potential future, she worries secrets from her past will one day find their way out into the open. How can she confess that she harboured a trace of regret she never made more of an effort to get with Simon - and that, as she sees him now, the larger part of her is glad she did not? Or that the way Sebastian treated her that summer for a while ruined her in terms of her relationships with men? Perhaps she is ruined still. No, the future is safer ground.

"I suppose I'm most worried about not being able to cope without Sharon. I think I took her too much for granted, and probably never realised what she gave me, her role in my life. And now I'm about to find out exactly what that was. It's wonderful that you've all come here - for me as much as her - but in consequence I'm expecting to be hit that much harder once you've gone."

As Judith places a hand on Niamh's arm they all fall silent. Niamh hopes this is more out of respect for Sharon than concern as to how her own future might pan out. But she cannot be certain. And then she is struck by how her simple statement seems to have deflated them all. Becoming downbeat could never have been the intention of Judith's challenge, so she feels guilty for having let them down - and thus burdened with the responsibility to pick them back up again.

"Is this supposed to be another one of those attempts to secure the last brownie?" When they laugh it is more an expression of relief than anything else. Having pulled them back from the brink, Niamh pushes them on. "If so, then it's someone else's turn now. Alan?"

With the die now cast, Judith glances at Sebastian. She has made her confession already, and having done so finds she is intrigued by what Sebastian may soon say. Although his gaze is fixed on Alan, she senses he will be trying to deconstruct the original question to work out a response. He may need some prompting.

"Okay." Alan holds them for a moment. "Well if I can't choose any of the conventional dying stuff it will have to be something else." He smiles briefly. "I think I *had* been scared about something to do with Sharon too, though I doubt I could articulate what that was with any clarity - at least not in the concrete way Niamh has. Maybe I didn't even know what it was myself; perhaps, even after all this time, a loose end I was scared I wouldn't be able to tie off... Now that she's gone I'll never be able to do that, and so I suppose there's no reason to fear it, is there? Just the fall-out. But as for everything else..." And suddenly it is 'everything else', as if he is staring into the vast expanse of the universe, his future potentially accosting him from any direction. "Emptiness." The word upon which he settles fits with the image suddenly in his head. "I guess I worry that in the end, when I look back, I'll find I've lived an empty life. I won't have had your kind of adventures Jude, nor a family like yours to console me, Simon... Will I end up staring into the mirror - and all the way back to 1988 - and wonder what it was all for and how it might have been different?"

As the gloom begins to descend, Sebastian - not entirely ignorant of his connection with Alan's regret - tries to leap into the breach.

"Jesus Christ, Alan, lighten up! Such a feeble attempt to get your grubby little paws on the brownie!" Hardly original, yet it is a joke which secures the desired reaction. Jude picks up on the theme.

"And, a bit like all those things we disqualified for Niamh, I suggest we're going to need a rule which makes inadmissible any stuff about emptiness and worthlessness too because - unless I'm very much mistaken - we could each of us choose that as an easy way to opt out of answering the question."

"Metaphysical nonsense!" Sebastian ventures.

There is a brief moment when - almost as if compelled to do so - they calibrate the notion of worthlessness against their own existence.

"But we'll allow the comments about Sharon," Niamh says quickly, recognising how easy it would be for the evening to slip away from them. "After all, at least that seems pertinent."

Following a few seconds' silence, Sebastian ventures to the fore again, partly to ensure the pace doesn't drop any further and partly to buy himself a little time before it's his turn.

"So we need cheering up." He inserts a pause which is just a little too long. "Over to you Simon."

Everyone except Simon laughs. His slim smile demonstrates he appreciates at least part of the humour behind the comment, recognises the joke is on him; yet none of that is sufficient to rouse his mood. Already prepared, he has decided they have not yet earned enough of his respect for him to divulge what he is really scared of - a bad cancer diagnosis - and so he is forced to adopt 'plan B'. He glances at Niamh, then around the table. Damage limitation.

"Well at least having a family gives me an angle the rest of you can't steal." There is an ambivalent tone in his voice which means they cannot precisely interpret the core emotion behind the words he is delivering, a combination of sincerity and dismissive disinterest suggesting he is going through the motions just for them. And yet perhaps there is more to it than that; perhaps in his case the clues reside in his tone rather than the words themselves. "And so I worry about what could happen to them - accidents, that kind of thing. Which I acknowledge is a bit like what's already been said, but as I haven't applied those fears to myself I think they should be allowed to stand." He waits for a challenge that doesn't come. "And obviously I hope I'm around to see them successful and happy; all the usual stuff, I suppose."

Whether they recognise it or not, Simon's statement begs the question as to assessment of the current depth of his own success and happiness. Does he wish the same for the rest of his family because he knows what that feels like, or because he wants them to enjoy the things he hasn't been able to? Or is he is merely playing along because deep down he doesn't really care at all? If he were to be asked that question directly, at this precise moment in time, then he would protest that of course he cares. Yet only he knows how honest he would choose to be if the can of worms representing his satisfaction with life were to be opened. Consequently, it is a lid he desires to keep firmly shut - even as Alan tries to prise it open.

"What about the practical stuff?" Alan, sensing that Simon's heart isn't truly in what he has just said, tries to offer him a link to a place he assumes he might be more comfortable.

"Practical?"

"You know, the non-family things. I think it's fair to say we'd all assume you'd want the best for them."

Simon nods slowly.

"Well they don't have to worry - practically-speaking - if anything happens to me. I sorted all that out a long time ago, and so Dawn has no concerns on that front, if that's what you mean." Alan fails to confirm that it was. "What else is practical then? Work, I suppose. I wouldn't say I'm scared of anything there, not really. Of course I'd like to get promoted again - but if I don't, that won't kill me." Another glance to Niamh. "And getting the sack or being made redundant, anything like that... Well, we all have to face those threats in one way or another don't we, so why worry?" Yet of all the things he has said, it is this latter which rings least true. And how could it not? Simon knows his life would crumble without his routine of the seven-fifteen train, the office rituals, the swift pint on a Friday lunchtime, the interminable meetings, the opportunity to lust silently over the women in HR... Simon needs these things to stop him thinking, to enable him to get from one end of the day to the other, walking out of - and then back into - his house. And behind his front door? All in all, his life is like a scratched record on an endless loop.

"I'm not sure such a feeble attempt would win you the brownie even if you were the only person in the competition!" When Sebastian laughs, the others join in with a chorus of derisive comments and boos. Simon is forced to laugh too, and for a fragment of a second he gets a glimpse into the past they once shared. The placing of an order for coffees interrupts the flow - and then, when Judith speaks, the door is slammed shut on him.

"Okay Mr Smart-Arse," she points at Sebastian, "your turn. I'm not sure who's winning at the moment - I actually think it's me! - so you're going to need to pull something really good out of the fire."

"Has that ever been a problem in the past?" Sebastian asks with an exaggerated air of confidence. Somewhere close to the surface, his mannerisms shadow a resonance of his father: in the smile, the gesture, the slight rising note in his question. Learned behaviour - nurture not nature - which Judith is able to recognise better than anyone else. Glancing round the table, Sebastian reaches for the wine bottle then tops up his glass, satisfied he is about to demonstrate that Jude is not the only one who has a 'performance' in them.

"Nothing." He delivers the one word with certainty, then takes a pull on his wine as he surveys the table.

"What do you mean 'nothing'?" Judith is incredulous.

"Simply that. I'm afraid of nothing. And all that mumbo-jumbo about 'why are we here?' and 'what's it all about?' makes no difference to me either."

"Well, it appears we're in the presence of some kind of modern super-hero; someone who's bullet proof, incapable of damage or failure, and from whom disaster simply steers clear." Judith punches a laugh across the table which the others fail to fully endorse.

If Sebastian's aim was to get their full attention, he has surely succeeded.

"Remember the original question, Jude: 'what are you scared of?' - and I repeat my answer. Nothing."

"What makes you so special? I'm sure we'd all like to know."

The smile which greets Judith is delivered with the certainty of a man who - if he were playing chess - knows he has checkmate in three.

"It's perfectly simple really. On the one hand I have tried just about everything there is to try and therefore can think of nothing that would hold any terrors for me. And secondly, I have the rather splendid blue blanket of my father and his perfectly comfortable wealth upon which, if necessary, I can fall back - both while it's still his and also knowing that one day it will all be mine. Hence - again - 'nothing'. So I don't even want the fucking brownie!"

There is something both triumphant and defiant in his voice. He beams at them in turn with the smugness of an athlete standing on the top step of an Olympic podium.

"Interesting philosophy," Alan ventures.

"But you can't be serious, Seb?"

"Why not, Niamh?" Sebastian looks at her. "I'm perfectly serious - and I'm being perfectly honest. I've already admitted to the fact that my childhood was - in its own way - privileged compared to most of yours. And now I'm simply suggesting that I regard my future as similarly endowed. That's all."

"But that's a staggering position to adopt."

"Is it Simon? I don't see why." He empties his wine glass. "Look, I don't have a family, so I don't have the kind of pressures and considerations you do. My career - such as it is - isn't centred on my looking gorgeous all the time, so I don't have to worry about wrinkles and sagging." He winks at Judith. "And neither is it dependant on promotion or anything like that because, when you think about it, I don't really have a career at all. You talked about redundancy, Simon; I'm immune to that too. I really am. I simply don't care."

"But what about being alone?" Niamh thinks about what she said earlier, and how solitary Alan seems to be. And she can see Simon isn't entirely happy with his family life - though how much the cancer question is weighing him down she can't be sure. As far as Judith is concerned, it appears she needs to be emotionally 'attached' to someone, and probably most of the time. All of which makes her follow-up question inevitable. "Why should you be so different?"

"Am I different? Perhaps my philosophy is different, that's all. I'm not looking for anything earth-shattering in the 'romance department'. I'll admit that once upon a time my aspirations were closer to the norm" - he forces himself not to look at Judith - "but they're not any more. I can exist by myself if I need to. And, you may not realise this or agree with me, but from where I stand it's far easier than most people think *not* to be alone for a while, if that's what you want. The world is full of people longing for an attachment of some kind." At this point, Sebastian does look at Judith, though whether his gaze is intended to convey a message in relation to the point he has just made - or the one immediately before - she is unable to decide.

"How can you be so…arrogant?" Simon beats Judith to the punch.

When Sebastian's smile transforms into the most almighty burst of laughter, the others can only exchange glances as they wait for him to regain his composure. Niamh is suddenly grateful she was able to secure a table discretely away from the rest of the diners.

"Oh I'm sorry!" Sebastian theatrically gasps for air as he endeavours to calm down. "Arrogant? You don't get it, do you?" It is a challenge levelled at them all, so he looks at each of them in turn. "You think I've said I'm scared of nothing because I'm being cocky, don't you? Like I'm some big-headed prick who doesn't understand how the world works. Well?" Their silence confirms his deduction. "I hate to burst your bubble, but the reason I'm not worried about anything is not merely because I've tried most things, but because I've failed at them. At just about everything. How can life hold any fears for me if I've already experienced the worst it's likely to throw at me?"

The triumphant smile is back as he secures the dregs from the final bottle of wine. Simultaneously their coffees are delivered and they pass milk and sugar between them.

"The worst?" The echo comes from Judith.

"No. I still don't get it, Seb. I think you're going to have to explain that to us."

The way Sebastian looks at Alan betrays more than pity for his lack of understanding; hardly disguised, there is contempt there too. And why should he not feel superior to a man whose life is dull and whose woman he once stole so easily?

"Okay, I'll spell it out for you." He moves to stir his coffee but picks up and drains his wine instead. "Shall we start with the career stuff? The logistics centre; remember? Complete disaster! I was fucking useless - and when I landed a job in Liverpool I think they were grateful because that meant they didn't have to sack me."

"So what came next?" Alan again.

"Next? Something to do with the docks - I can't remember what the role was. I think they'd been impressed that I'd already worked in logistics. After that imploded I got a job with a freight forwarding company for a while. Similar story, though I did get to go overseas a few times, which was a bonus. And then? To be honest the rest of nineties was a little bit hazy. I tried all sorts of things; some of the jobs came via my dad's connections. For a long time I assumed there was a perfect job out there for me and all I had to do was hunt it down; but every new road was just a dead-end. At one point Dad got dangerously frustrated."

"And now?"

"Interesting question, Niamh." Sebastian smiles. "I suppose you could say that I'm in advertising or marketing. Because I've met a lot of people, know a lot of people - many not through work, of course - I seem to have built-up a reputation for being able to fix things, bring parties together. I don't know what you'd call that. A kind of dating service for business people."

"Really?!" It is impossible not to tell from her voice that Judith finds the notion incredulous.

"Not that kind of dating, Jude," Sebastian immediately assumes her response is laced with innuendo, "though there has been the odd occasion… If you ever need introducing to anyone…" He laughs.

"That," she says haughtily, "would be like the apprentice trying to teach the master."

Although not intended as a joke, they all laugh.

"So you see, I'm no good at business, at being an entrepreneur, or at holding down a conventional job. And it clearly isn't because I'm not bright enough. I'm just not wired that way. Hence, 'nothing'. I've no career, so nothing to lose, nothing to be afraid of." He pauses. "At this point someone usually says how jealous they are and how they wish they were in my shoes." Sebastian waits for such a comment. "Or if they don't say it, they're certainly thinking it."

And are they? He looks at Simon and Alan to see if he can divine a trace of envy.

"That's a shame, Seb," Niamh posits the contrary view. "I remember your leaving 'do' - the four of us because you were already away, Jude. What you've described certainly wasn't the future you seemed to be looking forward to then. Perhaps it's just me or I'm misremembering it, but I can't help thinking you were - I don't know - optimistic."

"And I probably was, I probably was. But that was just Fool's Gold in the end. Oh, it took me a while to recognise it, those failures of mine eventually teaching me all the lessons I needed to know. But now I'd argue that I'm more optimistic than ever. Which may sound strange given what I've just said, but there's something liberating in my nomadic professional existence." He smiles. "So, given I don't want the metaphorical brownie - and that I've done absolutely nothing to deserve it - I suggest we award it to Jude as she seems to want the damn thing more than anyone else."

They all look her way.

"Not so fast, Seb."

"Oh?"

"You've only given us half an answer."

"In what sense?" Sebastian lifts the wine bottle again to check it's empty then, resigned to his fate, turns his attention to his cooling coffee.

"We've had the professional CV," she observes, "shabby though it is. But what about the second part? You and people and romance etcetera. We know about your dad - who doesn't? - but aren't you going to spill the beans on Melissa?"

"Melissa?" Niamh, Alan and Simon provide a chorus.

Sebastian's face darkens.

"I've heard your summary," Judith pushes on, prepared to twist the knife, "but I know a lot of people too, Seb - probably more than you, actually - and at least one of those people knows your father. Or Melissa's father. There are other variations of the story…" Judith tries to sound apologetic. "I can't be held responsible for what I hear."

"Then I dread to think what you've heard - especially if the original source was Rupert."

"It wasn't pretty," she confirms.

Sebastian looks at the others: Niamh is frowning, Alan sitting slightly forward, and on Simon's face a look which could easily be interpreted as a smirk.

"Rupert is Mel's father," he says as if this is explanation enough.

When he pauses, Judith takes the opportunity to nudge him on.

"I could tell the story, Seb - but I don't think that would be appropriate, do you? And my version is likely to be inaccurate."

Having been painted into a corner, Sebastian knows the only way out of the trap is to unveil one of the chunks of his narrative he was intending to keep to himself. It's not - he tells himself - as if he has anything to hide, but telling them about Melissa... Well, it hardly strengthens his position.

"Rupert was a friend of dad's. I say 'was' because they're not so close any more... I met Mel at a party in ninety-one. It was Rupert's birthday and dad had been invited. I was down from Liverpool for the weekend so I went along. She was a striking individual: attractive, outgoing, intelligent. I'd messed around a bit, you know, but hadn't met anyone like her in a while." He glances at Judith. "There was an immediate chemistry I suppose. We started dating. Initially it was a relaxed, long-distance kind of thing; but then she started coming north more often, and I would go back home some weekends to see her. Work wasn't great - though you're not surprised to hear that - and, although I didn't know it at the time, dad had been talking to this friend of his who worked at a freight company; you know, the one I mentioned before. Their head office was down south and dad seemed keen on the idea I head back that way. As was Mel. Path of least resistance stuff on my part I suppose. So I changed jobs, moved; then Mel and I started living together. None of it had been planned - when did I plan anything?! - it just sort of happened. Behind the scenes, dad and Rupert were plotting, encouraging. They thought we were a great couple, perfect for each other; they'd mapped out this future. Rupert was loaded, so oiling wheels came easily and naturally to him."

"Especially your wheels," Simon suggests with a lack of charity.

Sebastian ignores him.

"I can't remember who suggested marriage - except I'm pretty sure it wasn't me."

"Unless you were conned into doing so," Judith suggests.

"As you say…" Sebastian's smile is a weak one. "So we got married. And for a while it was all fine; no difference at all really. But then Mel started talking about children. Dad thought it was a great idea, just what I needed to get me to settle down, to make a proper man of me I suppose. But I wasn't sure." He pauses to reconsider what he has just said. "No, that's wrong. I *was* sure; sure I didn't want any. Maybe that's when things started to unravel. I found I was as good at marriage as I was at being 'a professional'. I simply couldn't do it… A couple of years later during a trip to Italy with the firm I met a woman in a hotel bar… Well, it was easy. And I was hundreds of miles from home, so who would know? Not that I'm particularly proud of it, but when I strayed again during a visit to Belgium, I realised what I'd been missing." Sebastian pauses again. "No, that's wrong too. I realised the sort of life that suited me, that I was wired for - and it wasn't one centred on marriage and domesticity. After that the wheels fell off pretty quickly. Although he gave me a complete bollocking, dad stood by me - which is why his relationship with Rupert went south. The divorce was quick and relatively painless - for me at least. Dad may have sweetened the pot for Rupert, I don't know. We'd married in ninety-three; four years later it was all over. On reflection, the only thing that still surprises me was that I'd lasted that long."

Sebastian looks down at his cup which he then lifts from the table and then downs the coffee in one. When no-one says anything, he turns to Judith.

"Does that fit with what you'd heard?"

"Pretty much," she says flatly, "but it's better hearing it from you."

"Better?" Sebastian laughs. "That's an interesting notion."

"I'm sorry," Niamh says.

"Sorry?" Sebastian turns to her. "For what?"

"That it didn't work out."

"It was never going to work out, Niamh." He waits a moment. "And that wasn't the worst of it really. For a while afterwards things became a bit strained with dad; I suppose he thought I'd let him down. And then the job imploded. Not because of Mel, but because someone had grassed on my international 'doings'. I'd been seen behaving 'inappropriately' - Italy and Belgium I suppose, and a few other places after that. I'd clearly demonstrated I didn't conform to the image with which the company wanted to be associated. And who could blame them?"

"And you?" Alan asks. "What did you think about what you'd done, that whole period?"

Sebastian looks slightly bemused, as if unable to understand how Alan could possibly ask such a question.

"Me? I didn't give a shit really. Oh, at the time I did; I may even have been distraught for a while, who knows? But I soon reconciled myself to who I was and the life I seemed destined to lead. So I changed jobs, played the field - both in terms of work and women. And before you say anything, don't ask me if I was proud of that, of my attitude, what I was doing. Pride never came into it. I was just being me… That felt like a new kind of honesty, for me anyway."

The last phrase is almost delivered as a challenge, as if Sebastian is implicitly suggesting that unlike him, the lives the rest of them had been leading were, to a degree, dishonest in some shape or form. It is an accusation he levels at the tablecloth rather than any individual.

"That's an interesting notion of honesty." They look at Alan.

"Well here's something else then," Sebastian's tone is suddenly edgy, confrontational. "If you want to talk about honesty, how's this?" He leans forward and picks up the empty wine bottle. "This is what I'm really married to." He thrusts it forward for a moment as if wanting them to get a closer look at the offending article, then lets it fall back to the table with a thump. It rocks, but remains upright. "I've always liked the sauce, you know that. And I'm well aware I've had more than my fair share this evening. That was always going to happen, wasn't it? What did you say earlier about drugs, Jude? Well booze is mine. I don't know when I started to hit the bottle pretty hard - before, during or after Mel? Who cares? I was warned about my drinking twice by my GP in the early naughties, and then found myself in a kind of rehab in 2008."

"It obviously didn't work," Judith suggests, an odd blend of accusation and pity in her voice.

"No kidding!" Sebastian laughs to himself. "Drinking's the only thing I've ever been really good at." Then he pauses and offers a general wink as if cheekiness will haul him back from the brink. "Well, one of them."

"And now?"

"You need to ask, Niamh?" Sebastian gestures to the bottle and the space on the table where the others had stood earlier. "It's a real merry-go-round. Rehab, cold turkey, on-the-wagon, off-the-wagon. Rinse and repeat. And in case you haven't guessed, I'm currently off, though I expect the cycle will begin again within the next few months or so."

"That's sad, Seb."

"Sad, Alan?" queries Sebastian, shaking his head.

"It's not sad." They all look at Simon, struck by a certain rigidity in his tone. "I'm sorry, but it's pathetic really."

"Pathetic? Surely not." Niamh is clearly on a different page. "It's an illness, Simon; that's what it is."

"Illness? Weakness more like. You had the best start of any of us, Seb; the best opportunities. And you've thrown all that away."

"But if that's the case, then isn't that sad too?" Alan challenges Simon, as if Sebastian isn't even with them.

"Aren't you going to venture an opinion, Jude?" Sebastian throws himself into the mêlée. "After all, I suddenly seem fair game." Knowing she doesn't need to, Judith shakes her head. "Very wise," Sebastian continues, now clearly fired-up. "You can think I'm ill if you want to, but I'm not sad and I'm not pathetic - and I'll tell you why. Because for all its flaws and its failing to conform to what's supposed to be 'normal' or acceptable, my life is an honest one. I know what I am, who I am. Whether you like it or not is irrelevant. Whether *I* like it or not is irrelevant too. I see it for what it is - for what I am - and I'm playing the cards I've been dealt. I'm not following some stupid script that's been laid down for me, a template I'm supposed to follow; I'm not clinging to a faded dream, a dream of something that was never going to turn into reality in a million years. We may all be hamsters running around in our own individual fucking wheels, but at least I *know* that's what I'm doing. A failure and a drunk I may be, but at least I'm an honest one."

Sebastian drops his eyes to the table, looking to see if there is something he can focus on, to lift or drink or eat, in order to break the spell. He knows he has been harsh, not on himself but on those around him. Perhaps it was the drink talking, but even so he cannot see any way in which Simon or Alan are qualified to pass judgement on him. Hasn't he always bested them? Aren't they the biggest failures around the table? And what of Jude? There he isn't sure. She chose not to take the opportunity to wade in and have her say - which would have been easy point-scoring for her - and so

Sebastian wants to think that maybe she is almost as self-aware as he, and that she sees her life and her celebrity for exactly what it is. Yet even though he doubts that to be one-hundred percent the case and remains unsure from where his motivation to give her credit stems, he finds he needs to believe she sees all of it, through it, around it; that she sees where she has been and is cognisant of the pit into which she is in danger of heading. Only by doing so would that make her life as honest as his.

And if she isn't sufficiently self-aware? Who is there to rescue her?

"I'm sorry," he says, looking up. He tries to look contrite. "Sorry Niamh. That was uncalled for." She tries a weak smile. He goes on. "I wonder what Sharon would have made of that little outburst? Probably slapped my face I shouldn't wonder. And quite right too."

"Hear, hear."

Sebastian looks at Judith.

"She might have, mightn't she?" He smiles. "She would have told me not to be a twat - though knowing her, she might have found a way to prevent the whole scene from happening in the first place." No-one speaks. "But I tell you something else though; she would have understood what I meant about honesty. She would have agreed with me. How could she not? Of all of us, I think Sharon was the one whose eyes were the most open, who saw things for exactly what they were. I doubt she ever went into any situation without understanding the terms of engagement. Or am I wrong?"

"No, I don't think so," Niamh is clearly relieved at the change of tack, "but somehow you make her sound cold and calculating."

"She was never that, as I'm sure Alan would concur." Calmer now, Sebastian rebuffs Niamh's challenge. "In her own way, she could probably be as romantic as any of us - but she understood where things stood, how they related to each other. All of which means she was probably the best at making decisions because she was aware of the factors and nuances and threads and potential outcomes... The best at that, I suspect."

And whether they recognise it or not, Sebastian's premise is an endorsement of himself as much as it is of Sharon. When she cast Alan aside in order to embark on their brief encounter, Sebastian understands that Sharon explicitly knew what she was doing and why she was doing it. The fact that it lasted for less than a week would have come as no surprise to her, nor would its brevity have burst the bubbles of any dreams she might have been harbouring - because there wouldn't have been any dreams. She'd had a desire to find out what a relationship with him was like - albeit a brief sexual one - and so she'd engineered one, certain he was never going to turn her down, not under the circumstances prevailing at the time. Between the two of them, the encounter had been brutally honest. But for the others? Sebastian is aware how it must have appeared, that he had been cast in the worst possible light, the villain of the piece pursuing a desire to get even with Judith. But what if the rest of them had known it had been Sharon who had made the first move, who had broken with Alan for the explicit purpose of bedding him?

There is irony here. When expounding his belief in honesty, he did so knowing he was being dishonest; and somehow worse than that - and flying in the face of his assertion to the contrary - was the fact Sharon had been dishonest with them too. Would he have chased her down had she not cornered him first? He thinks not; doubts that, for all their fallings-out, Judith had pushed him that far. Had he realised that as soon as he had walked into Sharon's trap all hope for reconciliation with Judith was lost, re-embarking on their passionate cycle impossible? Probably not, though the true cost of his infidelity only became evident when Judith discovered it. He suspects the compounding betrayal with Niamh was almost insignificant, a rubber-stamping rather than a fracturing event. He had told himself both episodes had been victories, demonstration of his superiority over all of them: Judith, Alan, Simon, Niamh - and even Sharon herself. It was a secret claim made to endorse the narrative he had been building for himself. And now? Now, no matter what he said or how vociferously he protested, it felt like clinging to the wreckage.

"Shall we get the bill?"

Before any of them can respond, Judith's hand is in the air and the young waiter who served them earlier is immediately there.

"Bill please," she smiles, unable to stop herself from indulging in the universal gesture which accompanies such a request: a flourish of her right hand in mid-air as if it is holding a pen and signing a cheque. She anticipates the young man has never seen anyone execute the hackneyed manoeuvre with as much grace and elegance.

Looking back to the table she finds Niamh in conversation with Simon and Alan about the bill, and Sebastian with his head slightly lowered, his fingers fiddling with a sugar cube. How much had Seb once been like that young waiter? She likes to think that as a couple they had possessed a certain kind of élan, the experience of which - although she had not realised it at the time - probably proved an important part of her apprenticeship for what would come later. If that was indeed the case, had their partnering merely provided advanced training in terms of the physical - how to be, to look, to move - or in the emotional too? That could only have been the case if the lessons learned also majored on avoidance: what not to do, how not to behave, who not to fall for. Surely to categorise at least part of their relationship's curriculum as such would be to take far too negative a view; perhaps Sebastian *had* inadvertently inoculated her against falling into similar traps again. Or perhaps the two of them had set the bar so high she had been trying to emulate their shared experience ever since? If such a positive spin is a notion she finds hard to comprehend - never mind accept - the spectacle of the man now sitting across from her does nothing to aid her being reconciled to it. Although a part of her admires his honesty - a painful lesson he has evidently learned - she cannot but help regard him as more or less a shell of the man she had loved all those years ago. Should there be any surprise in that? Or surprise in the fact that - even given her assessment of his decline - once or twice during the day she has looked his way when his attention was elsewhere and felt a faint tingle, the residue of old emotions worming their way through the fog of the past to give her the slightest nudge. 'Once upon a time', they seemed to be saying.

"'Once upon a time' what?" she asks herself defiantly, stunned such decayed feelings should have the temerity to tap her on the shoulder thirty years later. There is no denying she had been smitten by him, head-over-heels with his physicality, his easy grace. Even that sense of arrogance, bestowed on him by his upbringing and the mystique of his father, added to the compound which made Sebastian irresistible. And there had been much about him she once wished would rub off on her too; she wanted to feel that swagger for herself, inherit his sense of superiority. Theirs felt like an alliance which would elevate her above everyone else and help her get to where she wanted to be - even if, at the time, she had been unable to articulate where that might have been. She had called it love; of course she had. And even when they were going through their dark times - the result of his natural attributes butting up against the duplicates she was trying to cultivate for herself, like magnets of the same polarity - even then she had not questioned her feelings for him, that they were meant to be together. Yes, they had bounced away from each other on occasion, but subsequently their re-bonding had been more intense, more violent, more passionate than before. It was only a matter of time - she had told herself - when the collision would be so violent that they would be permanently fused together. If there had been a dream of 'once upon a time' then that Fairy Tale fusion would have been hers - and the one which failed to come to pass. Sebastian had seen to that thanks to his tawdry affair with Sharon. Judith had never questioned the notion that their bond was unbreakable, never doubted that Sebastian had felt so too. And then suddenly there he was, upsetting the very nature of things; he might as well have turned off gravity. And what made it worse - now, suddenly, and after all this time - was that they had reconvened in order to pay tribute to the woman who had helped destroy what

Judith now realises may have been the only pure thing she had ever had in her life.

She is roused from her reverie by the arrival of the waiter who presents her with a small china plate on which sits a folded slip of paper and an apparently random number of individually wrapped mints. Judith plucks a sweet from the plate then gestures the waiter towards Niamh who already has her purse out.

The next few minutes are taken up with the usual activities associated with restaurant departure: the validation that what they have been asked to pay aligns with what they have consumed; the last-minute visit to the facilities; the resumption of aimless and insignificant chatter; the well-rehearsed gathering of belongings and putting on of coats. Alone in this first pursuit and initially surprised by the size of the bill, Niamh is able to reconcile herself to it partly through recall of the numbers of bottles of wine they seem to have consumed, and partly because it is Sharon's money she is using to pay for them. Six bottles for the five of them. She glances up to where Sebastian is now wrestling with the jacket previously hung over the back of his chair. Clearly he is not the man he was and surely no longer capable of sweeping her off her feet as he once had (during a moment of weakness!) in spite of her knowing giving in to him was the wrong thing to do, a betrayal of Judith. Which was so soon to be followed on her part by a not unrelated second. Her attachment to Sebastian is now tenuous, she realises. Perhaps it is that way for all of them, the only common link they now possess merely historical - the stuff of legends. She had been struck by his clarion call for honesty, and found herself wanting to believe in him as much as he seemed to believe in himself. Yet she remained unsure, not simply in lacking the certainty that he was capable of living up to what he was espousing, but whether she herself might prove to be similarly disqualified. Perhaps none of them were quite in the clear when it came to being honest. In their own individual ways they had professed something akin to honesty during the evening, yet now, as they began to shuffle and rise from their chairs, she wondered if - with the symbolic donning of their outerwear -

they were going to leave all that behind, their coats and jackets protecting them not only against the chill outside but also acting as a barrier to prevent any further honesty from escaping.

She shivers involuntarily and then looks up to find they are all staring her way. In her hand she holds a fold of twenty-pound notes, and it is only in looking down at them - at Sharon's money - that she is able to reorient herself. She laughs, counts out an appropriate number to cover the bill then, finding she has still more in her hand, adds one further note to the pile. As if expecting the amount Sharon left her would be precisely what was needed and thus leave her with nothing, Niamh stares incomprehensibly at the remaining notes before she folds them roughly and forces the little bundle not into her purse but rather burying them in the bottom of her handbag. Yet this is hardly 'out of sight, out of mind'; how can it be when Sharon has been there all evening, sitting at her shoulder, and when invoked variously bristling or humming contentedly? Niamh tries to divine what Sharon would have made of Sebastian's speech. How true would it have rung for her? As she follows them to the door where he waits, holding it open for her, Niamh is suddenly struck by the question of trust; not trust in the others - though that is undoubtedly open to challenge - but trust in herself. If Sebastian were, even in his current drunken state, to make a pass later - 'for old times' sake', he might say - would she resist? And is there not a part of her that might want to offer some kind of solace to Simon who, in spite of his boorish unattractiveness, is clearly unhappy and possibly dying? Where do such thoughts come from? She wonders if she has become so much alone already, and whether the prospect of a life without Sharon is suddenly hitting her, much as the cool evening air now does?

"So," Alan says as they come to a halt just outside the restaurant. It is an invitation for someone to instruct them as to what happens next, a role so often performed by Sharon.

"Back to Alberta for more coffee?" Niamh asks open-endedly, knowing Judith, for one, will be accompanying her. In a way it is a question whose answer will provide some measure of judgement on the evening.

"Not for me, Niamh." Simon answers first. "I've made the mistake of booking a relatively early train back tomorrow, I'm afraid."

"Schoolboy error," suggests Sebastian.

"You're probably not wrong," Simon concedes.

"So will we see you before you leave?" Niamh finds herself wanting no loose ends.

"Only if you get an early ferry across the harbour."

They laugh.

"I'm afraid I'm pretty much the same," Alan informs her somewhat sheepishly, "so I'd better make my way back over with Simon; we can keep each other from throwing up on the boat. All that wine!"

There is another laugh, a time-honoured book-end to close something out.

"I may ring you in the morning," Niamh says, "just to check you're okay."

"That you haven't drowned in some tragic accident mid-harbour."

"What about you, Seb," Judith asks, rather than responding to his joke.

"Yes," Niamh picks up the theme, "where are you staying?"

"Some pub just outside of town."

"And you think you're going to drive there? Now?" Judith is incredulous.

"What are my options? I suppose I could go and sleep on Simon's floor…"

It is a notion which amuses all of them except Simon who, for the briefest moment, fears Sebastian might be serious.

"Come back with Jude and I," Niamh says. "You can sleep in the box room. It'll only take me a few minutes to make the bed up in there."

"You may not need to bother," Judith suggests, "he might just pass out!"

"Ah, a romantic evening with two lovely ladies!" Sebastian exaggerates his enthusiasm. "What more could a boy want?"

"In your dreams!"

Judith's joke is sufficient to terminate the conversation. For a few moments they dutifully execute the necessary pleasantries in order to see Simon and Alan off - handshakes and hugs, promises to be in touch - and then Niamh, Judith and Sebastian watch as they walk away towards town evidently not talking, the space between them just a little too large.

"Shall we?" says Sebastian, and offers an arm to each of his companions.

Departures

Niamh & Simon

"You got back to the hotel okay?"

"Obviously."

In spite of the relatively limited distance between Alberta Avenue and the hotel, when it comes to her through her Samsung, Simon's voice is uneven, as if there is something obstructing with the signal. Yet other than the harbour's expanse of water, there is little to interfere, not that their respective signals travel in a direct line between them - or at least that's what she assumes, technology never having been her strong suit.

"The return journey was uneventful," he is saying, "the ferry was fine, the water smooth enough; there were no alarms or incidents."

"And no-one was sick," she jokes.

"And no-one was sick."

"What time's your train?"

There is a slight pause during which - even though she is sure Simon knows precisely when the train is due to leave - Niamh can imagine him checking his watch to once again work back from that time to reconfirm exactly when he should be checking out.

"In a little under an hour. I'm just having one final coffee to take away the taste of that awful breakfast and then I'll be on my way."

"Is Alan on the same train?" As soon as she has asked the question, Niamh is struck by how unlikely that is, even though it shouldn't be; after all they are both going back to London and, from what she recalls from the previous evening, pursuing similar timetables with their agendas diverging beyond that. She recalls her assumption - remaining unconfirmed - that they would arrive on the same train too, as if that were sufficiently authoritative for a repeat to occur on their departure.

"No." Simon pauses. "I don't know which one he's on other than he said there was something he wanted to do or see before he left. I don't think it's anything special; maybe just to go for a bit of a walk." Another brief gap. "And you know he was never quite as punctual as me; not as keen to be on-time."

Niamh is unsure as to the veracity of Simon's assertion. To the best of her knowledge neither of them were ever late for anything, so it certainly wasn't the case that Simon could be relied upon to be the first through the door, the first to arrive. Possibly the first to leave, yes.

"And how are you?" She tries to nuance her question.

Simon misses the connection to their conversation the previous afternoon.

"Fine. No hangover or anything like that - though I wouldn't be surprised to hear that Sebastian's suffering."

She glances to the hall then allows her mind to travel up the stairs to where the door to the third bedroom remains closed.

"He hasn't emerged yet."

Simon's short laugh is broken up by a sudden wavering in the phone signal. It comes to her almost as a cough.

"No, that's not what I meant." She tries the words again. "How are *you*?" Perhaps the extra emphasis will help.

"Me?" There is another stutter in the signal as if in step with Simon recalibrating, undertaking a quick spot of self-examination. "I'm fine. Last night took my mind off things to be honest - at least until we left you."

"And now?"

"Now? I don't know. There may be a message or something waiting for me when I get home; you know, the surgery might have called yesterday (they open Saturday mornings), or there might be a letter from the hospital. One way or another something's going to turn up soon enough. And then we'll see."

"I hope..." Niamh doesn't even try to articulate what she hopes. "You know."

"Yes. Thanks."

What did she hope? Not as much about his diagnosis and his tests as about the general prospect of him, his future. Even if unarticulated, Niamh is sure she'd had hopes relating to each of them before they'd spent the day together, and as she and Simon chatter inanely for a few minutes, she can't help but wonder if her post-mortem as to what actually transpired - and then what might come next - has already started. Is her phone call to Simon the first in the closing of four loops or the cutting of cords to sever herself from the past? And somehow it would not just be her closure but Sharon's too, as if Niamh were her friend's proxy, charged with the final shutting of doors. Wasn't there something about not being able to pass over to the other side until there were no loose ends left? Or has she just made that up? Patrick Swayze and *Ghost* pops into her head. Not that such fantasy is something to believe in, of course. She wants to ask Simon what he will do when he gets off the train, what it will feel like when he walks through the front door of his house, sees Dawn, slips back into his normal life. Is it so radically different from the life they had once shared, all of them? There were routines even then. There were always routines.

She is suddenly conscious her phone is silent.

"Simon?" she says, her tone that of someone checking the connection is still active.

"I was just saying I ought to be going."

Niamh imagines one door beginning to swing shut.

"Of course. Let me know what happens, you know..."

"I will," Simon's reply is flat and noncommittal.

"And if you want anyone to talk to…" For a second time she allows her sentence to fade away, assuming he will be able to append the appropriate final clause.

And then he is gone.

§

Simon

What had she meant? "If you want anyone to talk to…" what? Ring her? Ring someone else? Come and see her or ask her to come and see him? Simon looks at his phone accusingly as if it has deliberately withheld crucial information from him. More like betrayal then. But it isn't just that. There had been something odd about Niamh all weekend, a nuance he had been unable to decipher. Perhaps that too had been buried beneath the surface of unfinished sentences.

He glances to where his bag rests on the bed, waiting. Packed twenty minutes ago, it has been nagging him to make a move, telling him he might just as well be waiting at the station as here; indeed, that it makes much more sense to do so. And the bag seems to remind him that if he goes now he is certain to miss Alan coming back from his walk. Although Alan is booked on the subsequent train, Simon has already calculated when their paths might cross, the likely moments of peril. There is an awkwardness he wishes to avoid and leaving in the next few minutes will give him the best chance of doing so, his departure unmolested, his walk to the station a solitary one. Already he imagines himself waiting for his train to arrive, and even though he has a seat booked, he will revel in being the first to embark once it has been prepared for its return journey to London. He toys with the thought of upgrading to First Class; surely there is no reason why he can't treat himself? It might be a fitting end to the weekend and a way of drawing a line under what has passed. Even the past itself.

Whether he wishes it to be the case or not, already they seem dead to him - Alan, Judith, Sebastian, Niamh, Sharon - and if such a sensation were to excavate any guilt in him then it would surely only be in Niamh's case.

He busies himself with his bag and one final check of the room before heading down to the lobby, choosing the freedom of the stairs in order to avoid any potential entrapment in the now-functioning lift. Confirming he has had no 'extras' to settle, Simon propels himself through the checking-out process as quickly as decency allows, then bursts out onto the pavement. He pauses to take a breath; it feels like the first since he left his room. After a quick glance to confirm Alan is not in sight, he makes his way across the road and, heading for the station entrance, retraces his steps from two days earlier. Released into the freedom of fresh air and the company of anonymous passers-by, Simon finds himself unable to avoid undertaking an assessment of his old acquaintances. In Alan's case it is not that he has anything against him, but rather he has come to realise he simply doesn't much like him. More than that; he probably never has. Unable to deny there *had* been a time when they had been friends, he acknowledges Sharon as the catalyst for that friendship ending. Indeed, he finds comfort in having always known that. The weekend - Alan's presence and Sharon somehow looming over them all - has reinforced that knowledge, made it more certain. He finds himself not wanting to waste time mourning his loss of fellow-feeling toward Alan, and, in the same way, he is suddenly cognisant that he does not feel the depth of regret in relation to Sharon's passing convention probably demands of him. If he is drawing a line, it appears before him as thick and dark with both Alan and Sharon's names etched indelibly beneath it.

Not wishing to interrogate himself further as to whether his placement of Sharon in relation to the line is appropriate, Simon moves on and mentally scrawls both Judith's and Sebastian's names alongside. Nothing could be more clear-cut, though for different reasons. Irrespective of his confirming that he has never *not* liked Judith - even if she did somewhat summarily reject his advances that time - she has earned her place below the line simply because he doesn't understand her, her lifestyle, what motivates her. Simon does not go as far as to regard her as a puzzle however. He likes to give himself credit that he can see what she is about, what she is 'up to'; rather, it is her conscious decision to apply a veneer of celebrity to her existence which throws him. He can see no reason for it; after all, there is no obvious deficiency for which she needs to try and compensate. Not that the same can be said about Sebastian. In Simon's eyes, here is a man who is continually adopting and discarding masks, dipping in and out of personalities, embarking on one escapade after another, all in an attempt to come to terms with reality. Perhaps at times he was almost as vulnerable to being charmed by Sebastian as the next person, so it is difficult for him to profess dislike; his name doesn't sit beneath the line because of that, nor because Simon doesn't understand him. More fundamentally, Simon places him there because how can he respect a man who is so plainly unable to cope with everyday life?

Having arrived at the station and found what he judges to be the most appropriate place to stand on the platform, Simon looks out to where his train will emerge and waits. All the distant signals he can see glow red; from this direction, not instructions to stop but rather not to go. It is a concept others might unpack philosophically and linguistically, but in his case each signal represents a fact - as much as four names written beneath an imaginary line might do something similar. He tries to imagine their names in red ink (stop, don't go) and realises he has no desire to see any of them ever again - which in Sharon's case is obviously outside of his control in any event. And Niamh? Where would her name sit on his sheet of paper, and in what colour would it be written?

In the distance, a train emerges from beyond the end of the platform and - strangely silent - heads towards him. Simon picks up his suitcase.

§

Niamh & Alan

"I thought I'd see Simon at breakfast but I didn't."

"Really?" Niamh tries to sound surprised. "I spoke to him a little while ago, just before he was leaving. I got the impression he was keen to get going."

"Perhaps he's desperate to be home." It is a stock phrase delivered by Alan without any conviction.

"Probably." Niamh accepts his statement for what it is. "How was your walk?"

"My walk?"

"Simon said you were going for a walk - for old time's sake - though he wasn't sure exactly where you'd go."

Alan laughs.

"That's because I haven't been out! I wonder where he got that idea from? I don't think I said anything last night about going for a walk this morning." He pauses. "I may have done, I suppose. We did drink a lot of wine... But no; I got up a little later than I'd planned, had a leisurely breakfast, and now you've called. Not a single step outside the hotel - though thinking about it, that's not such a bad idea. Or would have been."

"Would have been?"

"If I'd thought of it earlier." There is a pause. "But I simply don't have the time now."

"Are you keen to get back as well?"

"To what, London?" The question is clearly rhetorical, so Niamh leaves it unmolested. "Not especially. I've nothing to get back for, just the rest of the day - and the prospect of another week pretty much like the last one."

Niamh is struck by the hollowness in Alan's words, in the manner of their delivery. His is a voice devoid of emotion, swathed in the negative.

"Is it so bad?" She asks.

"Is what so bad?"

"Your life."

Another laugh - a little softer this time.

"It's not 'bad' - not compared to the majority, I suppose. I know I'm lucky in many ways: flat, job, that sort of thing. But it's not what it could of been. Yesterday proved that once again."

"Really?" Niamh concedes that the day may have confirmed many things but she had not included Alan's misplaced life as one of them. "I'm sorry. It wasn't meant to be anything other than a celebration."

"Well some people have a very odd way of celebrating... Is it unfair to say that?" He doesn't wait for an answer. "I guess it was being reminded of Sharon again, and in such an immediate way - though it's not as if I haven't thought of her on and off for far too long anyway. Seeing everyone together again... It brought her back, made her close again. For me at least. But then that was the whole idea, wasn't it?"

Niamh wonders if Alan had felt her presence during the day as much as she did. Perhaps Sharon had chosen to take possession of them all one last time; perhaps she had somehow risen in the cemetery and dusted herself over them. One last practical joke.

"We were always going to react in different ways," she says, specifically choosing not to answer his question. "I'm sorry it made you a little sad."

Alan tests out another laugh.

"Look, it was great that you did it, Niamh - arranged it all, I mean. And it was interesting to see everyone again. In places, quite hilarious. But 'sad'?" He weighs up the word, Niamh folding herself into the silence as he does so. "Maybe. Maybe it was always going to be sad for me one way or the other. I'm not sure Sebastian helped... But hey, what do they say about drawing lines and moving on?"

"That's the challenge I think I'll be facing now."

"Well good luck. I've been trying to move on for thirty years, and I now discover that I'm not as far forward as I'd hoped... But who am I kidding?" He lifts his tone. "But you'll be fine, Niamh. You're much more sorted and robust that you give yourself credit for. We'll all slot back into our individual grooves - wacky though one or two of them may be - and just get on with it."

"But you need something to look forward to," Niamh suggests.

"Don't we all? That may be where Jude and Seb have the edge on the rest of us."

"Why's that?"

"Because it seems to me that, in Jude's case, her life is a constant waterfall of adventures and mishaps, each one both subtly different and strikingly similar to the last. I suspect no two Mondays are alike in Jude's world - and if that's the case, isn't she the lucky one?"

"And Seb?"

"Ah Seb..." Alan adjusts his perspective. "Almost identical in one way, yet the complete opposite in another - and only because he doesn't give a damn. Where Jude cares desperately, he's totally ambivalent… Can you imagine if they'd actually made it work as a couple? There would be murder in the air!"

Niamh laughs as if another balloon has burst, the accompanying loudness of the 'pop' surprising her. From where she is standing in the kitchen she suddenly hears movement upstairs, the sounds of a drawer being opened and closed.

"I think Jude's getting up," she tells herself, as much as she is providing commentary to Alan.

"Then I should let you go," he says. "But thanks again, you know… And you also know where I am, how to get hold of me. It might be nice to do something slightly less frantic next time."

After he has hung up Niamh finds herself looking at her phone wondering not only where his words 'next time' had come from, but also needing to decipher exactly how they had been spoken and therefore what Alan had actually meant.

§

Alan

He wonders why he chose to use those words - 'next time' - as if he were prescient, had an inside track on the future. Which he did not of course - other than to know the complete opposite was true and there would be no 'next time'. How could there be? On what pretence would they meet? Perhaps when another one of them was to die? But in its own way that was a ridiculous notion, not in the dying but in the idea that, of the five left, any one of them had strong enough links - posthumous or otherwise - to pull the rest back together. Alan wondered if he were the next to go who might mourn him. He could only think of Niamh - and that said more about Niamh than it did him. Niamh would turn up for any of them.

Which posed the reverse question as to who he would mourn. Not only who, but how. Lifting his small suitcase onto the bed, he opens it and begins to pack, dirty clothes across its bottom followed by his book and his toiletry bag, with those few things he had not worn - the 'just in case' clothes - spread across the top. It was probably a sub-optimal method of layering, of distribution, and he was sure others would be more expert on the best way to repack a bag; Judith for example, whose experience would surely have made her a master of luggage management. Alan wondered if a week went by when she wasn't packing or unpacking a bag of some description, on her way too or from a shoot, into or out of a relationship, or travelling to an assignation of some kind. Surely she would be too busy to mourn him, her excuse ready-made if a little disingenuous. As far as he is concerned they had never really connected, behaving like satellites orbiting other planets, his gravitational pull too weak to have any effect on her. In terms of excuse, Sebastian's would be similar - though his failure to attend any ceremony relating to Alan would be for the simple reason that he didn't like him. Alan had suspected as much from the very beginning. There was a scale by which Sebastian chose to measure other men - and it was one against which he trembled rather than registered. They had been polite enough with each other the previous day (or at least that was Alan's assessment), yet it had gone no further than that. Hardly a cause for concern, it was simply how it was.

If he had harboured hope anywhere, then it had been with Simon. They had been the best of friends for a while until Sharon intervened, and even though their last meeting in London had gone badly, Alan had embarked on the weekend with the vague hope that being reunited through her might somehow generate sufficient force to bring the two of them back together and reverse all the negativity that had gone before. It had been a hope he knew could not be tested too rigorously - and which crumbled in Franco's.

He scans the room, less to validate whether he has left anything behind but more in the manner of a man searching for clues, as if on the chest of drawers, on the small side table, or fallen to the floor by the chair, there might be something dropped or forgotten which, suddenly elevated in importance, possessed the power to answer all his questions. But there is nothing. And so he smiles, lifts the case from the bed, and walks out into the hallway.

By the time he is within a few yards of the station steps he has filtered out all internal and external noise and settled on the remaining unanswered question. He chides himself for indulging in all that nonsense about who would turn up for his funeral and, in turn, whose he would attend. And he recalls again his words - 'next time' - and is assailed by the same certainty which has possessed him since he drove away from the place all those years ago: he only ever had one 'next time' for which he longed; one that, if it had become increasing unlikely as time passed, was now nothing, an impossibility. Sharon could never take him back.

Sliding his ticket into the barrier to open its low-slung grey gates, Alan walks onto the platform and, in the manner of all travellers, pauses to find his train on the departures board, checking the platform from which it will leave and that it is on-time. His pause - as with those around him - represents a kind of pulse, one of the many heartbeats of journeying. Given he has sufficient time to spare, he takes the long way round to platform five, eschewing the nearby stairs in favour of a walk to the very end of the terminus and across the walkway, past the rail-end buffers on one side and the ubiquitous 'usual suspect' concessions on the other.

He had hoped Sharon would have come to see him off that first time he left. She seemed to have shed the after-effects of Sebastian readily enough and, from what he could see, had reestablished herself in a new skin. Perhaps that image of her provided a clue to his own problem - and which continued to be his problem - in that he found such a sloughing impossible. Walking past the Costa and heading along his platform, he is reminded of the afternoon when he tried to win her back, when he laid himself before her, devoid of any pretence - and probably of any dignity too - and just begged. Had that been a gambit which ensured not merely temporary but also permanent failure? Had he been more patient, given time a little longer to work its magic on her, might she have been more receptive? Or had he simply driven the inevitable last nail into the coffin of their relationship? Even now he likes to think not - in the same way as he had thought for all the years between then and now that he still had a chance, that one day the phone would ring or a letter arrive. That had been his only true 'next time'.

§

Niamh & Judith

When Niamh emerges from the kitchen she finds a fully-dressed Judith waiting for her at the foot of the stairs, her coat already removed from the coat rack and hanging loosely over her arm. Niamh follows the line of it down to where a suitcase stands to attention an inch or so from Judith's right leg.

"You're going," Niamh says, unnecessarily. "So soon?"

Judith's smile is an apologetic one.

"I have to get back to London for something this evening and I need to make sure I give myself enough time. I can't very well go dressed like this."

Her statement - and the laugh which accompanies it - is delivered as if she has provided all the information Niamh could possibly need to understand the nature of the event to which Judith is heading. Yet based on their encounter over the previous day or so, Niamh remains at a loss, only able to define Judith's upcoming assignation in vague and somehow inconsequential terms: it will either be a party, some other PR event, or a man. For an instant she is tempted to seek clarification, but decides there is little point. In any event, Judith is already furthering her argument.

"And to be honest, I don't really want to be here when His Lordship wakes up. It could be awkward."

Niamh is struck by the phrase.

"Nothing happened last night did it - I mean after I went to bed?"

Judith laughs abruptly, then, covering her mouth with her free hand, tries to smother the sound, glancing up the stairs as she does so.

"Heaven forbid!" The notion has clearly amused her. "That *would* have been a turn up!" She laughs again. "No; I suppose I just want to avoid - I don't know - any further risk of an inquisition. At times last night I thought he was heading that way."

"An inquisition?"

"On my life. On what we once shared - and what happened to it." Judith pauses. "Didn't you think he was…*critical*? I mean, not just of me, but of everybody. Him, of all people… I had the sense that instead of laying old ghosts to rest - if that's what the rest of us were trying to do - he was intent on digging them up, giving them a fresh lease of life. That is if you can dig up a ghost - which, of course, you can't. Anyway, something like that is the last thing I need. Especially when it comes to Seb."

Niamh looks away from Judith and around the hallway as if she has somehow failed, as if the house - hers and Sharon's house - has been complicit in that failure. And she thinks of ghosts and what she has wanted to say for the last twenty-four hours.

"But won't you have any breakfast?" It is a weak ploy, knowingly insufficient to extend Judith's stay.

"I'll get something on the way. There's a drive-thru on the way out of town; I'll probably grab a coffee there. It's sad of me, I know, but I do have a weakness for corporate mochaccinos!"

Although she wants to protest, to offer sausages, bacon, the best coffee she can muster, Niamh senses the futility of doing so. From somewhere she imagines a clock ticking down Judith's departure.

"Before you go…" She pauses. Judith, sensing Niamh's hesitancy, shifts her posture slightly, standing just a shade taller. It is a gesture that holds Niamh back, makes her feel less signicant.

"Yes?"

"There's something I've been wanting to tell you. Or rather wanted to tell you yesterday." Niamh struggles. "In fact, something I should have told you years ago."

"I'm intrigued."

"It's about Seb."

Judith laughs.

"I doubt there is anything you could tell me about that man I don't already know. Or if I didn't know, that would surprise me."

Niamh takes a half-step back and hopes it goes unnoticed.

"You know he had that thing with Sharon, just briefly. After you split up that last time."

"Of course I do." Judith's smile is open and unconditional. "Doesn't everyone? I think we were almost done by then anyway - though I have to admit when I found out it sealed our fate. It probably helped me decide my own. Perhaps in an odd way Sharon did me a favour." She pauses. "I never felt sorry for me. Not really. Alan was the one who suffered the most I think."

"He still does."

"Does he?" Judith considers the assertion. "Maybe he does. But should he? I don't know. I wouldn't have. And I don't."

The last phrase strikes Niamh as being slightly out of kilter with what Judith has said, at odds with the tone she has been trying to strike. It is a notion that almost holds her back.

"And with me."

"And what with you?" Judith tilts her head to one side a little patronisingly, almost as if she is trying to understand what a child it saying.

"Seb had a thing with me too. Right after Sharon."

Judith glances down to her coat, to where her other hand rests on the bannister.

"You knew that too, right?" Niamh wants her news to not be news at all; she wants it to be a repeat, like and re-run of an old black-and-white movie.

"Knew it? Not specifically, but I had my suspicions." She perks herself up, suddenly on the verge of motion. "But like I said, we were over by then. The fact that he tried it on with you..." Judith takes a moment to process the idea. "Well, that's so typically him then, isn't it?" Another pause. "And I'm sorry."

It is a sentiment floating in the air looking for a home.

"Sorry?"

"For you. I don't know what it would have been like... Exciting probably; unexpected, adventurous, flattering. All those kinds of things. And I should know. But was it really? Really? Seb has a way of cheapening things, don't you think?" She pauses. "But you'll have your own theories I suppose - and your own feelings. So if it's forgiveness of some kind you're after then you don't need to worry on my account. I already had one foot out of the door by then anyway."

And as if taking her words as a cue, Judith takes two steps forward to give Niamh a perfunctory kiss on the cheek.

"Forgive yourself, Niamh," she counsels, "but maybe don't forgive him." Again Judith casts a glance upwards. "And don't worry about me."

Niamh stares at the back of a front door deliberately closed by Judith to prevent her from standing on the threshold and watching her guest's walk to the car, the loading of the boot, the driving away. There will be no waving, no hugs, no tears. If it seemed an unemotional departure, Judith's words resonate for perhaps no more than a short while. Niamh tries to gauge whether she had been worried about Judith or not, and comes to the conclusion she had not. What was there to concern her? Certainly they were both wrestling with something, but Judith's daemons were of a different ilk to Sebastian's, in a different ballpark altogether. How could it be possible for Niamh to concern herself about someone moving in a sphere she simply could not comprehend? If Judith had meant for Niamh not to be concerned about her and Sebastian - either as individuals or as a residual couple - Niamh was as certain as she could be that there was no danger of that. Or perhaps fifty-percent certain.

§

Judith

Slotting the takeaway beaker into the vacant cup-holder, Judith finds herself just a little disappointed that she had not been served by the young man from two days earlier. It would have been an opportunity to give her departure a lift. There had been no recognition at all in the somewhat glazed expression of the woman who had taken her order, her eyes betraying that she was either at the end of a long shift or had deliberately disengaged her brain, running on auto-pilot to get through the day.

Whilst her arrival in the town had some intrigue about it - the marvelling at changes, the assertion of memory and history - leaving felt entirely different; it was as if she was not only closing a chapter, but an entire volume. And not merely closing it, but consigning it to the flames. She knew - as well as she knew anything - that she was leaving behind nothing which mattered to her. It was a harsh assessment of course, but one bolstered by her appreciation of the roadsigns as she made her way out of town and onto the motorway; the destinations on offer were once again filled with promise and opportunity - and all because they weren't pointing toward the place from which she had just escaped. There was a moment - brief but precious - where she recognised her supremacy, an ability to rise above everything, and that this act of driving, her being alone in her car speeding along in the outside lane, seemed a demonstration of that supremacy. It was proof, if proof were needed; her life was filled with choice and the freedom to exercise that choice. Had she wanted to she could turn off at the next junction, head east or west, north or south; she could investigate new places, try new things. She felt unbound and for a moment it was wonderful.

Yet it was a freedom that came at a price, a coin with a second side. Judith found herself considering the others from the perspective of having roots, things to look forward to. Yes, it was obvious that Simon and Alan hated their lives (for different reasons) and Niamh had her work and enjoyed the structure it gave her - though how her life might come to feel with the ballast of Sharon removed was unclear. Did Judith care? She felt a little sorry for Niamh because she was the most decent and honest of them all - a consideration surprisingly untainted by the somewhat ham-fisted confession made at the last possible moment, presumably to minimise the pain of any future repercussions. Judith consoled herself (if consolation was needed) by pretending she had known about Sebastian's second infidelity even before it had happened, and believed herself when she told Niamh the two of them had been finished by then anyway. Perhaps both were true. However, her hatred for Sharon remained unspoken, as did her unswerving belief that, had she not set her cap at Sebastian - and for such a tawdry little affair! - the two of them would have reconnected again, the cycle resumed. That hatred, trumping everything else, casting its long shadow across her history, was the reason why there was nothing from which Niamh needed absolution, and why Judith found she could forgive Sebastian his indiscretions - even pity him. After all, he had become a man with nothing to look forward to at all. It seemed to Judith that even the opportunity to turn left or right was denied him, so fast was he stuck in the ruts which ran in the shadow of his father's greatness; his was a life which was spiralling towards some inevitable and shabby conclusion. What did Sebastian have to believe in? Nothing. None of the rest of them did. All of which made her position so much the more superior. Yes, under duress she would confess to having had the odd 'wobble', minor crises which always seemed to work themselves out; but by and large she possessed the one thing none of the rest of them had nor could understand: an unshakeable belief in herself.

Something makes her glance in her rear view mirror and she sees, from some way back, the unmistakeable outline of a police car closing on her. Indicating appropriately, Judith steers into the middle lane and begins to moderate her speed; then she repeats the sequence again. By the time the police car zips past her she is only marginally over the speed limit, glancing out of the door window to offer the motorway her most demure smile, just in case. There are no sirens, no blue lights, and the officers of the Hampshire Constabulary roar away into the distance. She smiles to herself as she regains the middle lane and increases her speed. There had been more than one occasion when there *had* been blue lights trained on her - and once when her smile, the offer of a signed photograph, had allowed her to escape with a warning. But that had been how many years ago now?

Those were the kind of memories Judith found herself relying on more and more these days; evidence of triumphs, of her rightful place in the world. Wasn't that sense of belonging - and of being valued - another example of her supremacy over the others? Surely that was set, secure; she felt as if she had cemented herself in the grand scheme of things. Did it get any better than that? Which of the others could make such a claim? Certainly not Alan, Simon or Niamh, who lived their lives at the beck-and-call of others, mere cogs in some vast machine. And not Sebastian either; he who had proven himself incapable of finding an environment prepared to tolerate him. Yet in amongst all this triumph there was suddenly something else. As she overtook two lorries each proudly brandishing the livery of a corporate giant, she was struck by the notion of belonging, not in the sense of the world in general but in the microcosm offered by family - corporate or otherwise. Certainly Simon may hate his life, but he has a family to fall back on, to belong to, whether he detests them or not. And she finds herself supposing that, in their own way, both Niamh and Alan are attached to a 'family' of sorts; their work colleagues, their daily chores, the environment in which they spend a third of their lives. And Niamh spoke fondly of Siobhan, her sister, and their Irish roots. Even Sebastian could - at a push - be given some credit for remaining attached to his father and associated entourage whether or not the relationship was mildly dysfunctional; at least it was there. Looking at her life through that particular lens, what did she have that was comparable?

It was an uncomfortable question. Oh she had tried - was still trying - to find such an attachment, but at times it felt an impossible task. She tells herself that as a child she had been corrupted by her mother - and later by her relationship with Sebastian - and as a result had been banished from joining the 'attachment club'. Now there was nothing she could do to gain anything other than temporary membership. Judith shakes her head as if trying to shake away a bothersome fly. How can she think that way when she has already proven her superiority?

She tries a smile, then leans a little harder on the accelerator and races away from the lorries she has just overtaken.

Niamh & Sebastian

The image presented by Sebastian when he appears framed in the kitchen doorway a few minutes later couldn't have been more in contrast to Judith's neat preparedness. He looks as if he'd had an argument with a duvet and come off second best. Niamh glances up at him across the rim of the mug containing her second tea of the morning.

"There's tea in the pot," she says, as if that were all that mattered.

"Thanks. Any chance of a coffee?" He looks around the kitchen as if scanning for signs of the enemy. "Where's Jude?"

Already on her feet and heading for the kettle, Niamh replies over her shoulder.

"You've just missed her."

"Gone already?"

"She said she had something to get back for." Turning, she catches a glimpse of Sebastian as he rearranges his face into a more neutral expression, unable to read what had been there before. "Is instant okay? We just about finished the ground last night."

"Did we? I'm not sure I remember." He checks himself. "Or rather, I didn't realise. Sorry."

"No need to apologise."

She busies herself with a jar and spoon, introducing a heap of Gold Blend into the bottom of a mug; once they had arrived back the previous evening she discovered when it came to Sebastian and coffee there was still no need for milk. After a short pause, the kettle boils again and she pours water onto the granules, stirs, then lifts the mug from the work-surface. Occupying the seat opposite her own, Sebastian is at the kitchen table skimming through the newspaper she had been reading.

"That's yesterday's of course," she says, placing the coffee in front of him.

"Is it?" He questions the assertion as if she has put forward a weird notion, either in the existence of 'yesterday' or the passage of time altogether. "It doesn't matter; I don't really keep up with the news, so it could be last week's and I'd be none the wiser." He smiles, then takes the coffee from her, cradling his hands about the mug. "Thanks."

"Did you sleep alright?"

"Out like a light I suspect - though that spare bed of yours seemed really narrow. Cold too."

"Really?" If there was any inference in Sebastian's statement Niamh misses it. The back bedroom is one of those rare spaces in the house which is always warm, summer or winter, whether the radiators are on or not. She has always found its claustrophobic nature soothing, protective; more than once in the wake of Sharon's death she had allowed herself to sleep in there, wanting to be cocooned, cradled. But this is not a confession to be shared with Sebastian.

She watches him as he flicks through the classified ads, suddenly overcome with the desire that he should be gone; she wants to go up to the bedroom in which he slept and strip the bed, wash the linen, hoover the floor - almost as if she were performing an exorcism.

"So what are your plans for today?"

Sebastian looks up, a slight air of surprise in his eyes. She wonders if he has been taken aback at her question or brought up short by the notion that she might think he would have any plans at all.

"I need to get back to the pub and pick up my things. Even though I didn't sleep there I expect he'll still want to charge me... Seems odd that I'll have to pay for him looking after my stuff." He considers the prospect. "Maybe I'll be able to get a discount - seeing as how he's my dad's mate and that I didn't have breakfast. Talking of which…"

"There's toast and cereal, and that's about it." Niamh catches a look in Sebastian's eyes. "The bread's in the bin next to the toaster and the cereal's in the cupboard next to the fridge. Help yourself. I have to put some washing on."

She doesn't of course, but the need to escape has overwhelmed her - though she is unable to say whether the desire is brought on by the thought of acting as waitress or being confined with Sebastian in the kitchen. It could also be a sudden and unbidden flashback to that one morning thirty years earlier when the two of them had sat opposite each other across an earlier incarnation of the table, one wondering what the future might now hold, and the other already knowing the answer. How had he looked back then? Had he appeared as dishevelled and unkempt? If so, then Niamh knew she had been at least partly responsible for how that morning had found him. How it had found both of them.

Whether it is tactless or not, Niamh makes her way upstairs and strips not only the bed in which Judith slept - Sharon's old divan - but also that in the back room, opening curtains and windows in both bedrooms to let fresh air in. Or is it to let something out? Lifting the lid on the hamper in the bathroom, she drops as much of the linen as possible in there, carrying the remainder downstairs, through the kitchen and into the utility room where she busies herself with the washing machine.

"Did she say anything?" Sebastian speaks as Niamh emerges back into the kitchen.

For an instant Niamh imagines he is speaking of Sharon, as if she has been able to convene with her in the few minutes since she abandoned him.

"Judith?" she asks, as if clarification is necessary.

Sebastian nods.

"About what?"

"Anything."

What had she said? Niamh recalls their brief conversation at the foot of the stairs, her clumsy confession, how Judith had reacted; she places Sebastian in the context of that exchange and how they - she and Judith - had chosen to refer to him.

"Nothing really. Only that there was something she needed to get back to London for and that's why she was getting away early."

"It seems she always has something to get to," Sebastian says somewhat wistfully. "Or away from."

Niamh allows a brief pause to settle.

"Perhaps that's what her life is like," she offers, "full of things that put demands on her."

"Demands?"

"To be somewhere - or to not be somewhere. She certainly makes the rest of us seem humdrum, don't you think? In terms of the lives we lead I mean…"

As Sebastian takes a moment to consider his response, Niamh escapes again, this time heading into the lounge, looking for further examples of her guests' presence, other things she needs to expunge. For the next few minutes she busies herself with the unnecessary - like fussing over cushions and coasters - all the while listening to noises filtering through from the kitchen: a cupboard opening, the toaster popping, the kettle being refilled. Her actions are the complete opposite to how she was at their only other breakfast together, presaging of those few precious hours when she was unwilling to have him out of her sight.

Pausing by the front room window, she looks out onto the street and sees his car parked across the road behind the space Judith had filled. Soon enough that space would have doubled in size with Sebastian on his way back into his own crazy life. She is glad he will soon be gone, the representation of the past he offered filled with nothing but conflict: what might have been, but wasn't; what shouldn't have been, but was. There had been a well into which she had cast all emotions related to their entanglement; guided by Sharon, it had been the only way she could move on. How far she'd moved had always been open to question, however. Hadn't James proved as much? Wasn't he, in his own way, a reincarnation of the Sebastian who had so casually ruined her? And if he had been an echo of sorts, how much stronger and louder was the sound now, given Sebastian himself sat just a few feet from her, eating her toast and drinking her coffee? Niamh realises that her experience over the previous twenty-four hours has seen her swing like a pendulum to the extremes of emotional attachment, a transit thirty years in the making. Standing at the window, watching the paperboy deliver the Sundays to number thirty-three, she wonders if that pendulum had ever threatened to swing back in Sebastian's direction - or might yet do so. Perhaps it is now she is at greatest risk. Perhaps that is why she wants him gone.

The sound of a chair being pushed back returns her from her reverie; she hears the dishwasher being opened, a mug and plate being loaded. She waits for his voice to assault her, but there is nothing more than the sound of him padding through the hall and then up the stairs. Back in the kitchen, Niamh finishes tidying things away - the dirty knife, the butter left out of the fridge - then wets a cloth and wipes the table, the work-surface. Unplugging the toaster, she takes it to the bin and pulls out both crumb drawers, tipping their contents away. Even the crumbs have to go.

Looking around the kitchen, Niamh is struck by how many things have associations, not merely from Sebastian's recent transactions but from Judith too. If she is prepared to go back in time (as she seems to be) then those associations must include Sharon, and earlier versions of both Simon and Alan. And even herself. Even herself. There is suddenly much to exorcise.

§

Sebastian

"I'll see what I can do," Tommy says a little dubiously in answer to Sebastian's request for a further discount. "I accept you didn't have breakfast, but I'll still have to clean and service the room after you've gone."

"Thanks Tommy," Sebastian says, as if the Landlord had already acquiesced. "A quick bath and then I'll be off."

"Heavy night, was it?" Tommy's question hits Sebastian in the back just as he is about to leave the empty bar and go to his room.

"Heavy?" Sebastian weighs up the question knowing there are multiple ways in which 'heavy' can be interpreted. The usual inference - especially from a publican - would relate to having had too much to drink, an outcome which may, in his case, be all too evident. Yet in this case he suspects Tommy means something else: had he 'got lucky'?

Although the answer is indisputably in the negative, it is a question to which Sebastian returns once stretched out in the rather generous bath his spacious en-suite is able to accommodate. There had been a time - indeed, occasionally there still *were* times - when the measure of a successful evening was not to wake-up alone in the morning. The previous day had not fallen into that category for several reasons, the primary of these being that Sebastian hadn't embarked on the evening with either Judith or Niamh on his mind. At least not in that way. Too much like revisiting the scene of past crimes. Having said that, he had flirted with them on and off, yet not in earnest nor with any premeditated intent. Being 'chatty' and engaging was all about who he was and how he was made, so how could he not? In advance of the meal he had been fairly certain that neither of the ladies in question would have been particularly receptive to pursuit, though there were moments when he thought he interpreted the odd hint... Certainly Judith was looking stunning; more so than he had imagined she would be. Over time he had watched her progress with interest - from the perspectives of both detached observer and as the partner of a woman he had once loved - falling into the lazy assumption that as she aged her beauty could only be maintained thanks to increasing quantities of make-up and potentially the odd invasive treatment. There was, of course, no evidence of the latter and, if he were honest, not much of the former either. Perhaps he should have drunk less and focussed a little more after all.

He glances down to where the bubbles have begun to thin across the surface of the water and catches a glimpse of his penis lying limp against the top of his left thigh. That little chap was, quite obviously, another story. 'Percy' had, over the previous few years, proven increasingly less performant, even to the extent that he had experienced the odd embarrassing occasion when he had found himself resorting to the legendary excuse of "that sort of thing doesn't normally happen to me". And it didn't. Or hadn't. Ever since he had made the requisite youthful discoveries and emerged from a relatively short period of trial-and-error, Sebastian had always been proud of his sexual prowess, not merely in terms of his strike rate in seducing women, but in his stamina, his technique, his ability to make them happy. Yet in spite of his track record, his reputation, all three abilities now seemed to be on the wane. What if Judith *had* fancied a reprise 'for old time's sake'; how would he have managed? And given she was still in pretty good nick, how might any subsequent failure to measure-up have reflected on him? He tells himself he would have risen to the occasion, that Percy would not have let him down; yet there is the nagging doubt that, no matter how hard he tried, he would have failed to meet her expectations of him, expectations based on their shared history.

The drink wouldn't have helped, obviously. Historically it had never been a problem, booze and sex proving happy enough bedfellows; but these days he wasn't so sure. He wondered if drink was beginning to impact on him in the 'trouser department' too. Enough people had warned him about the effect it could have on his health, but to the best of his recall no-one had suggested a link between it and loss of sexual potency - at least not in his hearing. Or was degraded performance simply an age thing? Was what he was going through - a slide into sexual mediocrity and presumably worse beyond that - nothing more than his body beginning to down tools, a road along which all men must travel, even his father? Such a prospect being something of an anathema to him, he could only hope not; yet even as he tried to dismiss the thought, to reassert notions of supremacy and invincibility which had been his steadfast companions over the years, Sebastian knew he would do well to avoid the truth for much longer.

Truth? Cloudy memories of his outburst during the meal came back to him. What was it he had said? Hadn't he talked a little bit about his drinking, his lifestyle? Although he had rattled on about honesty, he was fairly sure he hadn't mentioned sex. What possible reason would he have had for doing so? Not only had he wanted to maintain his superiority over Alan and Simon - which hadn't been difficult - he had also been keen to not surrender any ground to Judith; it would have been totally unacceptable for her to have left the restaurant with any sense that she had one up on him. If he excused Niamh as not really counting, Sebastian knew Judith was the only real challenge.

Which was something Sharon had been, of course. He is surprised she has come to him just then, and he slides beneath the surface of the water for a moment as if to wash them all away. But when he sits up seconds later she is still there. Sebastian is struck how little they seemed to have spoken of her across the weekend. Yes, there had been the trip to the cemetery and a few minutes of reflection imposed on them, but after that? He has a vague notion of Niamh trying to steer them in Sharon's direction whenever she could, but there was too much of their individual selves getting in the way.

Standing up, he leans for the towel he had placed on the rail nearby and begins to dry himself. The water having failed to rid him of her, he tries to rub her away; heading back north devoid of any residual trace of them the only acceptable outcome. For a short while - and in a very real sense - Sharon had been very much attached to him. Sebastian remembers the period as lasting a few days only; certainly less than a week. He recalls her sudden advance, his guard down having recently split from Judith again. He chooses to revisit himself as a man in some turmoil, wanting to reconnect with Judith but - for the first time, perhaps - unsure how to. If he had been swamped by Sharon's sudden full-frontal attack then, even so, his capitulation still came easily enough - and Percy had certainly been anything but unwilling! There was something almost animalistic about her assault which surprised him, and she had not left him alone - or rather, they had not left each other alone - for probably forty-eight hours. Whether he ever questioned what it was they were doing or why they were doing it - whether the 'truth' of it ever came into question - he cannot say. If he were now to be filing those days away in some dusty cabinet, he would probably look for folders marked 'inconsequential' or 'opportunistic' in which to deposit them. Their liaison had been more than inconsequential of course, and with Sharon being remarkably dismissive when their brief flame went out, its repercussions proved the most significant for Judith and Alan. He has recollections of feeling unaffected and impervious - and of choosing to demonstrate as much by bedding Niamh at the first opportunity, just to prove a point. Inconsequential and opportunistic most definitely. But where was the benefit in him raking through those cold embers now? The weekend was over, nothing much had happened.

As he dresses, he tries to look forward but can only imagine the drive north. He sees himself in his car, glancing in the rear view mirror only to find the faces of Judith, Sharon and Niamh taking turns to stare back at him. He would like to be able to interpret the expressions on their faces, individual clues to truths with which he feels they expect him to be familiar. He smiles and shakes his head. Well, he thinks to himself, if they're all in the rear-view mirror then that's the best place for them, and he imagines himself putting his foot down to get away from them as quickly as possible.

§

Niamh & Sharon

An hour and a half later Niamh emerges from the kitchen with another cup of tea and heads for the lounge. The washing she had put on earlier is now in the tumble drier, the kitchen surfaces have been cleaned, the breakfast things washed-up, and she has prepared a list for her trip to the supermarket later. In addition to refreshing her stock of ground coffee, she has managed to identify one or two other items where she is running low. As a reward for getting through the previous day she might even buy herself a treat of some kind having always had a soft spot for chocolate eclairs and Eccles cakes.

Placing her cup on the coffee table, she eases herself into her favourite chair; to her left is the sideboard - which has recently begun to double as a bookcase - then the television, the fireplace, and to the right of the window the small sofa on which Sharon used to sit, more often than not her legs tucked underneath her. When she was concentrating - on either the tv or Niamh herself - she might choose to wear her glasses, one of her few concessions to ageing.

As Niamh looks up from her first sip of tea she imagines Sharon sitting there.

"That went well," Niamh hears the spectre say.

"Do you think so?"

"At least it's over."

Sharon is smiling, and Niamh realises how much she has missed her friend even though she has only been gone a few weeks.

"You're looking well," she finds herself saying, not bothering to challenge the fact that someone who isn't there could 'look' anything at all.

Sharon laughs. "I find my present situation lends me a few advantages... I thought about being a little younger - you know, photoshopping myself - but that didn't seem appropriate; you might not have approved."

"Approved?"

"You might have thought I was taking advantage of you."

Niamh looks away to the window, shaking her head somewhat sadly. When she looks back, she is surprised to find Sharon still projected on the sofa.

"Anyway, at least you're finally rid of us," Sharon says.

"In what sense?"

"In the sense that you don't have to worry about us any more, nor any of that nonsense from the past. Those unanswered questions."

"Were there questions?"

Sharon laughs again. "Listen to yourself! Weren't you around yesterday or was I watching someone impersonating you? Oh, the things you discover!"

"But I didn't think I needed to be rid of anyone," Niamh protests, returning to Sharon's assertion, "least of all you."

"Probably most of all me!"

Niamh wants to tell Sharon that she can't conceive of a scenario where her life would be better without her friend in it, but there is something in Sharon's demeanour, the way she is smiling, which suggests that - as ever - she knows better. Trying to find a word to describe what she is seeing - real or otherwise - Niamh settles on 'aura' though she knows it is woefully inadequate.

"And I'm rid of them too," Sharon adds.

"You?"

"Don't you think we've done them a favour, Niamh? That over the last day or so we've managed to close a few chapters, draw some threads together, tie things off? You choose the terminology, after all you were always the literary one." Sharon pauses, glancing to the books on top of the sideboard. "Though having said that, you *are* choosing the words, aren't you?"

When Sharon laughs, Niamh feels a tear slip down her cheek. So that's what this is, she says to herself.

"Of course," Sharon confirms, "that's exactly what this is. And for the other three too - though in a different way..."

Niamh lifts her tea to her lips once again, wondering what her next move should be - and knowing that any next move *is* hers, even to the extent of being able to stand up and simply walk out of the room. But that would be too radical, too brutal; and Sharon hasn't yet finished, that much is obvious.

"I was a little disappointed," Niamh begins, testing out the phrase to see if the Sharon she is imagining will pick up on it, knowing - better than she does herself - what the words mean and what might lay behind them.

"Disappointed in?"

"Where do I start?" Niamh offers a smile which combines the wistful with the regretful. Had she truly been disappointed? Her desire to see them all gone, to rid the house of traces of Judith and Sebastian surely said something else. And the others too?

"Simon?" Sharon suggests. "He would seem the least incendiary."

It is an interesting choice of word, but Niamh lets it go.

"I don't know," Niamh lies. "He seemed so old, so empty; as if he'd been hollowed out by life. A shell of the person we once knew."

"And you're surprised?"

"I said I was disappointed," Niamh corrects her friend, "which is something else entirely."

"Is it?" Sharon seems to mull over both concepts for a moment. "I was neither. There were signs - even all those years ago - as to how he would turn out, what would become of him." She pauses to allow Niamh to interject, but she does not. "You might not have seen that in him as clearly as I did, I suppose, but you saw it nonetheless."

"Really? How?"

"In my case it was especially clear when he made his declaration. I have never known the word 'love' to sit on anyone's lips as uncomfortably as it did on Simon's that day."

"Isn't that a little cruel?"

"It was as if he were trying to sell me an insurance policy, or asking me to provide the cover for his life. I think even then he had an inkling as to the kind of man he really was, how his future would turn out; and I think he wanted me to stop that from happening. Or if not to stop it, then to at least provide him some comfort as he got older and life disappointed him. Or he disappointed himself."

"He's got Dawn," Niamh suggests.

"And you think she's doing that job?" Sharon's tone is momentarily dismissive. "Not that it's her fault probably. You heard him, you saw how he behaved."

"But his cancer?"

"Which he may or may not have," Sharon clarifies. "Don't forget that." She pauses. "And if he has - I say *if* he has - then Simon's the kind of character who was *always* going to get cancer. For him it would be the ultimate proof of how shitty life is. He would be vindicated."

"Now that *is* cruel."

Sharon's gaze is unwavering, seeming to transmit the truth in everything she knows - or reflecting back to Niamh everything *she* knows.

"But you saw them too, those signs of how he would turn out. Have you ever asked yourself why you and he never made any real effort to connect?" Sharon doesn't wait for a response. "Don't answer that; I'll tell you. It was because you knew; deep down you could see how things would turn out... You ask me if that's me being cruel. But is it cruel or honest? Wasn't honesty the big topic of the weekend? And wouldn't you expect me to be honest? Wasn't that what you said - what everyone said? It's nice to be seen as a paragon of something positive, even if the attribution is a little misplaced."

"Misplaced?"

Sharon's laughter reminds Niamh of evenings after the pub, of Sunday morning walks, of inspecting the fall-out from bizarre culinary experiments.

"You think I was always honest? Really? Is anyone?" There is a short pause during which Sharon examines Niamh's face. "Don't give me that look of shock, Niamh; you're not a child. You know how dishonest people can be - for Christ's sake, you've only got to think of James! But the headline news is that we were all at it, especially back then - not that my dishonesty is something of which I'm particularly proud." A cloud crosses Sharon's face. "And you know it could be worse than simply that."

"How so?"

"A cocktail of dishonesty mixed with something else - and not something that would redeem it."

"Such as?"

"Self-interest."

Niamh is unconvinced.

"You'll need to provide me with evidence."

"Are you sure that's what you want?"

Considering her options for a moment - which are so obviously limited - eventually Niamh says "Do I have any choice?"

"Very well." Sharon pauses a fraction of a second. "Alan."

"Alan what?" Niamh is unsure where this is heading.

"My relationship with Alan. Triggered less by any notion of love than to get back at Simon, to put him in his place, to demonstrate to him what a failure he was - or was going to be. He'd insulted me. It was the least I could do..."

"But..."

"But nothing. Oh, don't get me wrong; I really liked Alan, and it was nice being a couple with him. He had lots of great qualities: was kind, caring - all that stuff. And he did what he was told too."

"You make him sound like a well-trained dog!"

Sharon allows a gap to build before she next speaks. "He was never going to be 'the one' - if you believe in that kind of thing. In the beginning his most attractive feature was that he wasn't Simon. He was also available, of course; and though I hadn't really been looking for a relationship, Simon got me thinking - and maybe I should thank him for that."

"But Alan was devastated when you broke up with him. He's still devastated. You knew he'd always harboured the hope that one day you'd ask him back. He may not have been 'the one' for you, but I think he was in an entirely different place…" Niamh tries to juggle what she now knows with what she has always believed, getting herself into a tangle where both intertwine as if they were actually one and the same all along.

"But that was never going to happen, me being happy to take him back. Remember, I knew what that looked like from the other side."

"I think it may have been the one thing that kept him going, that vague possibility. What happened between you two…well, it defined his life."

This time Sharon's laugh has a harder edge.

"You believe that? Really? He could have been whatever he wanted - within reason, of course. As could Simon. As could any of us, I suppose. But to put his faith in a relationship that was never, for one moment, exactly how he imagined it, how he idealised it… That was why it was so easy to throw him over for Seb. An entirely different prospect."

"But that's so callous."

"Is it? Or honest? Or that nasty mix of being cruel and self-serving? It's your choice, Niamh; you can make of this what you want - literally. I'm just unpacking it for you. And the simple fact is that Seb posed a different kind of challenge; an irresistible one."

"We used to think he wooed you away from Alan."

"Yes, that was the only logical conclusion to be drawn wasn't it, based on the evidence, the back catalogue as it were. But he was closer to the truth yesterday evening wasn't he - even if such honesty cost him a little personal something."

Remembering the exchange, Niamh had thought it brave.

"Brave? Possibly." Sharon doesn't sound convinced. "But I wanted to see what all the fuss was about - and what Jude saw in him, given his track record and the fact that the two of them couldn't make it stick. Why not let someone else have a go? Not that I was in it for the long haul, you understand. I think the evidence demonstrates as much. I just had the sense that I might be able to - I don't know - 'tame' him, get him under control, rescue him from the person he seemed destined to become. Call me sentimental, but I thought there might have been something worth saving."

Niamh shakes her head. "Based on this exchange, sentimental is hardly the first word I'd use."

"There!" Sharon sounds a triumphant note. "I'd said you'd be glad to be rid of us all!"

"But you didn't tame him, as you put it." Niamh feels as if it is about time she fought back. "It was all 'wham-bam, thank you-ma'am', and then it was over."

"Because he couldn't be saved. It was obvious. Even after one evening, one night. He'd pressed the self-destruct button long before I got involved and there was no way to stop the count-down." Sharon glances toward the window. "But there is one thing I regret and one thing about which I'm happy."

"Really? Surprise me."

There is suddenly something softer in Sharon's smile, as if it is laced with regret for the first time.

"We're nearly there," she says, her voice a little quieter, more subdued.

"Nearly where?"

"Nearly at that place where you'll be happy to let me go, so that you can get on with your life…"

The cup on the table catches Niamh's eye. It is empty, but she can't remember finishing the tea. Perhaps she should get another, but getting up and going back into the kitchen would surely break the spell.

"We should just finish this first," Sharon says. "Before you go and put the kettle on again. Don't you think?"

Niamh makes the effort to sit up a little straighter, as if to demonstrate that she's maximising her attention. And then, to prove she was listening, echoes "one thing you're happy about, and one thing you regret".

Sharon's wistful smile returns.

"I'm happy that it ruined his relationship with Jude. Not for his sake, you understand, but for hers. I like to think I was responsible for setting her free. Not that I liked her that much - which I now understand was entirely mutual. She was always too full of herself, too much the 'I am'; too pretty, too clever - too good in bed I shouldn't wonder, though Seb never said. She was probably too everything come to think of it… Didn't you get that? Don't you get that still? Little Miss Perfect - except she isn't, of course; far from it. But then that's pretty obvious to everyone, isn't it?" When Niamh doesn't respond, Sharon presses her. "Tell me I'm right, Niamh."

"You're right."

There is an uncomfortable moment before Niamh speaks again.

"And your regret?"

"Look, no-one's perfect. And although I could see lots of things - about Simon, Seb and the rest, I couldn't foresee everything."

"Such as?" A pause. Niamh presses. "Sharon?"

"I had no idea that he'd rebound from me straight into you. Seb, I mean. I thought Simon might try it, and I knew Alan wouldn't; but Seb? If anything I thought he'd just go back to Jude so they could start on their stupid merry-go-round again. But he didn't. Jude had seen through him by then too; slammed the door on him. Which left him only one option before he moved on. As if to get back at us all." Sharon pauses, waits for a response of some kind from Niamh. Then she resorts to "I'm sorry".

Niamh looks away to the window then down to her hands. She feels as if she is holding something tangible in them; the sensation suggests a combination of materials, wood and metal, a heaviness. It is an artefact she is unable to materialise, yet she stares at her fingers as if it is there, as if she could caress it.

"Well you may be off the hook," Niamh says eventually. "Because that may in fact have been my doing."

"How so?"

"Because all those years ago I was the one who first told Jude about Seb's fling with you; because I wanted to - I don't know… Maybe I thought he'd mistreated you, abused your friendship. I wanted him to pay. So it could have been me who forced that door shut, me who was responsible for giving Seb the need to find somewhere else to seek solace after you'd dented his pride. I was the only one left. I'd wanted to hurt him and in the end it backfired onto me. It all backfired onto me."

And now Niamh suddenly knew why Sharon had been such a rock after Sebastian had violated her; it had been driven more by guilt than fellow feeling. And she also knew that his preying on her had occurred because of her own desire for revenge. Niamh feels another tear fall and looks down expecting to find a pool of them in her lap. But there is nothing there, and the imaginary instrument has vanished from her hands. And when she looks back up, Sharon too has gone.

Acknowledgements

I need to express my gratitude to film-maker and screenwriter Stephen Nesbit who, when this book was little more than an idea - and when I was struggling to get beyond the first few thousand words - made a number of suggestions in relation to processes I could try to adopt in order to get some momentum behind its writing.

I should thank Jan Birley for her running of the writers' retreat at which - as part of the overall event - I was introduced to Steve. And thanks also to Rebecca and Hamish, and their Garsdale Retreat, the oasis at which the bulk of the editing of this book took place.

www.writersretreatuk.co.uk

www.thegarsdaleretreat.co.uk